Altered Perspectives

Bible Stories from an altered viewpoint

In *Altered Perspectives,* Philip Levin, M.D., writes a fascinating new modern Midrash on the Torah. Midrash is an ancient Jewish tradition going back to the early rabbis of filling in the gaps of the stories of the Hebrew Bible. The author does this masterfully.
– Rabbi Donald Kunstadt, Springhill Ave. Temple, Mobile, AL

Without taking anything from the Biblical account, these new viewpoints strengthen our understanding of the history surrounding the stories.
– Reverend Joseph L. Cutshall, Gulfport, MS

To my dear friend Elaine —
a very talented writer —
May your spirit be inspired —
& fearless —

Philip Levin
July 2013

First Edition: February 2013

Published in the United States of America
By Doctor's Dreams Publishing
PO Box 952, Long Beach, MS 39560
www.DoctorsDreams.net

ISBN: 978-0-9834396-7-7

Cover Photo by Philip L. Levin, MD

Library of Congress Control Number:
2013930529

Altered Perspectives

Bible Stories from an altered viewpoint

Esau: The story of Jacob and Esau told from the "other" brother's viewpoint.

Zipporah: Moses' decision to abandon his family on a quest to liberate the Hebrews in Egypt told from his wife's viewpoint.

Based on original Torah (Old Testament) Scripture.

by Philip L. Levin, MD

Story One: Esau

Prologue:

Rebekah peeked into the tent's flap; *just a quick glance*, she told herself. Inside, the soothsayer hunched over a boiling cauldron, its heavy fumes filling the tent with a mysterious odor. Without looking up, the hag motioned for the girl to enter and sit on the stool. Rebekah started to back out, wishing she hadn't given in to her friends' taunts. But really, what was the harm in a childhood prank? *Twelve years old, is still a child, right?* She took a seat on the stool.

The old woman cackled, and Rebekah grabbed tightly to the stool's seat. "Shalom?" she called hesitantly.

"I know what you wish to hear." A gold earring glittered off the light of the cauldron's fire as the old woman gazed into the pot. "Yes … yes. About marriage, nu?"

Rebekah squeezed her hands together tightly. She didn't really believe; that's what she kept telling herself. But … it would be so fun to hear. She put her hand in her purse and brought out the silver coin, clenching it tightly. "How much?"

The old woman's face rotated into view. Rebekah shrank back at sight of the solid white eyeballs, their lids red and sagging. Wordlessly the soothsayer held out her hand and Rebekah placed the coin in its outstretched palm. The fist closed tightly and the woman brought the coin up to her mouth, biting hard. Her pale lips opened in a broken-toothed smile.

Gazing back into her pot, she used both bony hands to waft the aroma into her face, her breathing sonorous. When she spoke her discordant words floated like autumn leaves, journeying on a breeze. "A strange fate awaits you. A man from afar will summon you to live as the mistress of a holy home."

Rebekah clapped her hands, her pigtails dancing as she wiggled with joy. "Will there be children? Will I birth a big family? Please tell me. Please say yes."

The old woman gave a gentle stir to the bubbling cauldron, releasing sickly sweet aromas. Rebekah settled still and held her breath.

"Your voice just turns with the juices of womanhood," the Soothsayer murmured. "Yet you dream of siring a great family. In truth I see your lineage will be the founding of two great nations! Twin sons."

"Twins!" She'd known only one set of twins who had survived childhood. Already this sounded grand.

The old woman held up a finger. "Twin boys. One will be dark, one light. One evil, one good. Both will found mighty nations, which will forever be at war."

Rebekah stood up, sending the stool flying back against the hut's wall. "War? My sons create great nations just so they can fight each other?" She kicked the metal pot, producing a dull thud. "How DARE you say that to me! This was supposed to be fun!" She turned abruptly, her nose high in the air. As she walked out she muttered, "It's a good thing I don't believe in these things!"

Chapter One: Genesis 25:27-34

Esau had been tracking the wisp of smoke for the past few leagues, certain who he'd find. Peering out from behind a wild olive trunk, he spotted his quarry. Thirty yards off, his brother squatted over a pot, his back turned. Esau decided he'd try sneaking up on him.

Crouching, he took two steps into the opening, stopping abruptly as a brown head rose from the grasses a dozen paces ahead. The dog snarled, and Jacob turned abruptly, breaking into a laugh.

"You should see your face, Esau!" Jacob clicked his fingers and the dog ran back to his side, raising his head to receive the reward of a few head pats. The creature settled at Jacob's feet, but kept his watch on the newcomer.

Esau started to walk up to his brother, but the dog stood and bared his teeth. Esau snorted. "Teaching Kelev to hate thy brother, eh?" He settled onto a rock and watched Jacob stir the metal cauldron. Its roasted garlic smell caused his empty stomach to growl.

"What's cooking?" he asked.

Jacob didn't look up from the pot. "It's not for you."

Esau looked across the prairie to his parent's compound, a couple of hundred paces up the hill. The ground had been well cleared, a sturdy boundary of thorn bushes encompassing the half dozen stone huts. This had been his home his whole life, fifteen years, though now that he had family with the Seirs, he wondered how much longer it would be.

"Come on, Achi," Esau cajoled. "There's plenty in that pot and I haven't eaten in a couple of days."

"'Achi'? Don't cajole me with that brotherly love crap." Jacob stood up, holding the dripping spoon in one hand, the other on his jutted hip. "Gone for five days and what'd you bring us with those legendary hunting skills you're always bragging about? You got a venison you need help hauling to the house? No? A string of rabbits? No? I didn't think so."

He turned back to his work, giving the porridge a good swirl which produced a cloud full of sweet vegetable smells. Esau leaned forward, inhaling deeply. He licked the salivation off his lips.

"I had other things to take care of."

Jacob banged the pot with the spoon. "Yeah. I know what you were doing. Seeing your little Seir bitch. It's disgusting."

Esau felt his face flush. He stood and took a threatening step towards Jacob, stopping abruptly when Kevel raised his head and growled. Esau lowered back onto the rock. Plucking a reed, be began nibbling on it. The aromas coming off the cauldron were driving him crazy.

"Stop teasing me, Jacob. I'm famished. Let me eat some of that red pottage."

"Nope. This is for Father and Ishmael."

"Uncle Ishmael's here?" Esau stood, contemplating going up to the compound to greet him. Ishmael was a great hunter and storyteller and would have all sorts of news.

Esau's stomach growled with emptiness. Craning to peek in the pot, he said, "There's plenty here. You know you're going to give me some when you call the family down here to eat. Give me my portion now."

Jacob picked up his walking stick and held onto it for support as he stretched his back. "It's lentil stew. I don't suppose you know what that means?"

"We eat lentils all the time. Just give me some stew, God damn it."

Jacob glared down at him. "Don't take the name of our Lord in vain."

"Sorry." Esau sighed. "So tell me, oh wise brother who has lived the same fifteen summers as ignorant me, what does lentil stew mean?"

"It's a meal given to the bereaved. In this case your father." Jacob pointed to the compound above. "While you were out consorting, your grandfather passed."

Esau hung his head and pulled a rip in his cloth. "Abraham passed? Wow! It's like ... like the moon stopped rising. I mean he was older than dirt, but still..." Esau turned to his brother, "When did he die?"

"Yesterday afternoon; Ishmael came to fetch us. We all leave in the morning to go to the funeral."

Esau rubbed his right wrist's fur spot, thinking of the times he had sat around the evening fires listening to Abraham tell stories. Esau's favorite had been the one where his grandfather had broken all the idols in his father's shop. Heh. *And they call ME rebellious.*

A gentle breeze brought another whiff of the soup to his nose. "What's it going to take for you to give me some lentil stew?"

Jacob lifted the spoon and took a sip. He mimicked an expression of ecstasy and smacked his lips. "Yummy!" He shook his finger at his brother. "I've been taking care of everything around here; organizing the shepherds, monitoring the crops, and with mom's help, taking care of Dad. And you're – where? Shacking up with a Seir whore?"

Esau shook his fist at his brother. "Don't you go calling Adah a whore. She's the mother of my child!"

"You don't live with her."

Esau thought of the clan he'd just left. The Seirs were good people, a branch of the Canaanites who loved to party. They'd invited him to join their clan, but he hadn't decided. He sure couldn't see bringing Adah and little Eliphaz to come live in the Hebrew camp. He reached down and doodled some in the dirt.

Jacob picked a wood chunk from a nearby stack and stuck it on the coals. Pointing at the simmering cauldron, he said, "If you want some of this stew you're going to have to buy it."

Esau snorted. "What's your price?" He opened his hip bag and pulled out an animal tooth. "How about this? It's from a lion. Always brought me good luck."

"No." Jacob concentrated on his stirring.

Esau sifted through the bag. Finding nothing else of value he stood and looked towards the compound. It was only a quarter league up the hill. He could probably find something to eat there, maybe some dry fruit or grain. It sure wouldn't be as good as this steaming stew with the delicious aroma. "Well, what DO you want, then?"

Jacob put the spoon down and settled back on his haunches. Eyeing his brother carefully, he said, "My price is your birthright."

"What?"

"You agree to tell father that I deserve to be given first inheritance rights. Just because you were born a few heartbeats before me shouldn't give you birthright. You're never around. I have to make all the decisions around here anyway. I deserve the birthright."

Esau laughed. "For a bowl of porridge? You're joking."

"What do you care? You'd rather be off bedding girls and getting drunk."

"You think you're all so hot? I'm perfectly capable of running a household. I've got a family now, you know."

"Look," Jacob said. "It won't change anything. All I'm asking is for you to agree to tell Dad I'm getting the birthright, and you can have all the stew you want. I'll still be here doing all the work and you'll still be off … doing whatever it is you do."

Esau considered. *What was a birthright anyway? It wouldn't feed you when you were hungry. It didn't stop you from having a family with another clan.* He looked up towards the camp. *It was scraggly. Isaac had taken over a piece of land unwanted by the Canaanites, so rocky the goats had to be grazed on land several leagues off. Besides a few itinerant shepherds, staffed by an aging man nearly blind, a woman of nearly forty summers, an ancient nursemaid, and two teenage boys, all trying to exist in the middle of nowhere for the sake of a bunch of hooey beliefs. I'd be better off marrying Adah. Elon would grant me a generous piece of land as a dowry, and maybe even a serving wench or two. That Timna was a real cutie.*

What's here for me anyway, especially with Grandfather dead? Father loves me, true, but Mom's always showed preference for Jacob. And look at the way he's treating his one and only brother who wouldn't even give him a bowl of food when he was hungry without giving him a dressing down. Maybe it was time to move on.

Jacob scooped up a spoonful of the stew and placed it in a wooden bowl. He waved it in the air, fanning the aroma in Esau's direction.

"What difference does it make what I say?" Esau asked. "Passing of the birthright is up to Father. You know he prefers me."

"You have to tell him."

Jacob walked the few steps across the clearing and held the bowl under Esau's nose. The older brother closed his eyes and took a smell. He held up his hands and Jacob lowered the bowl into them, stepping back to the pot to give another stir.

Esau settled onto his rock and blew across the bowl's top to cool it before taking a gingerly sip. The brew was every bit as delicious as he'd expected. As quickly as he could he downed the bowl and licked the insides clean. Bringing it across to Jacob, he said, "More."

Jacob looked down in the bowl and up at his brother. "Look at this. It's full of your hair. That patch on your arm is as hairy as the baboons that wreck the fields. I bet you're not really Father's son, but some baboon crept into the cave and slept with our mother."

"And you're as pale and bald as the baboon's ass, and twice as ugly. Give me more stew before I kill your filthy cur and dispense with your head." He pulled out his knife and waved it in Jacob's direction. The dog stood at attention baring its teeth.

"Stay," Jacob told the dog. He flashed Esau an ingratiating smile. "I was just kidding. Here." He wiped out the bowl, refilled it, and handed it to Esau. He also gave him a piece of bread.

Esau settled back onto the rock and resumed his eating, more slowly this time, savoring the flavors. "Strong with the garlic, aren't you?"

"You need it, Brother. Custom says garlic cures jealousy."

"Then you're the one who needs it. Birthright, my foot."

"With Grandfather dead and Ishmael here, Father's bound to be thinking about his own mortality. When he talks with you, you have to tell him you've given me the birthright."

Esau didn't reply, taking his time with the second bowl as he considered. *I made the promise, but, really, should I actually do it? This place wasn't much, but it is home. Maybe I'd best wait and see if Dad makes any comments after the funeral.* He finished this second bowl and tossed it to Jacob, who swished some water in it and placed it inside his cooking bag.

"Where are we going to bury the old man?" Esau asked.

"In the cave where they buried Grandma Sarah, near Adah's home in Hittite."

Esau glanced towards the east, remembering the striated river bed with all the caves. "That's Ephron's land," he said. "He's important in the Hittite clan. Grandpa used to own those fields east of Mamre. Heck, it's less than a day's hike from the Seirs. Seems to me Father should be glad I've taken Adah so our family has ties with them."

"Father doesn't mind Adah. In fact, he seems to like your little brat. Ever since you brought them to visit last month he's talked about him all the time. It's just … you know, she's a Pagan."

Esau shrugged. "Seems to me there's no way of knowing whether there's one God or many." It was an old argument between them, one Esau loved to use to irritate his brother.

Jacob glared at him, then reached down and pulled a bell from his bag. Holding it high above his head, he rocked it back and forth until its sounds echoed across the pasture. Esau watched as ten people emerged from the huts above and began the trek down the hill towards them. He easily picked out the regular inhabitants of Isaac's homestead, his father and mother and the old nanny, Kaymah. Two more were the itinerate shepherds. The other five all were dressed in the blue fringed white robes of the Hebrew tribe. When they got closer he recognized his uncle Ishmael, gray-haired and wrinkled, but still with figure lean and strong.

Esau admired Ishmael. *Grandmother Sarah's jealousy drove Ishmael and his mother away when he was a teenager, yet he still keeps in contact with the family. Strange; Isaac married someone just like Grandma Sarah; just as mean, just as conniving, just as vicious. Maybe Jacob has a point. Why would I even want to visit this place after father dies?*

Sitting down on the rock again he took another sip of the water, thinking about the wine of the Seir camp. *They have such great meals; the women love pleasing their men, and everyone's happy and prosperous. What do I need my silly birthright for, anyway?*

Chapter Two: Genesis 27 Introduction

Kevel growled, drawing Rebekah's attention. His teeth bared, his nose pointed down the hill. Behind him, Jacob, in half-stoop, shaded his eyes as he peered over the row of bean bushes. Rebekah ducked beside him, waiting on her son's report.

"Two on camels, a man and a youth." Jacob kept one hand on the dog's collar. "It looks like the cloaks of Ishmael's clan. Kevel and I will go greet them. You want to go tell Father?"

Rebekah considered. "No. Let's take them down to the arbor in the lower meadow. Best find out what they want before we bring Isaac in on it. If they're friendly, I'll go ahead and lay out some refreshments."

She remained hidden, watching her son and his dog go up to greet the travelers. In moments they drew Jacob into friendly hugs and cheek kisses. Satisfied, Rebekah hurried down to the creek's edge where the family had built a small gazebo with garden table. Dipping a pitcher into the creek, she pulled out fresh water and set it on the table with a bowl of nuts and olives from yesterday's pick.

Jacob led the two men into the shaded arbor and made introductions. "Mother, this is Massa, Ishmael's seventh son." Indicating his mother, he said, "Massa, this is Rebekah, Isaac's wife and my mother."

"Welcome my cousins," Rebekah greeted. "You must quench your thirst, sate your hunger. How is Ishmael, Massa? I have not seen my brother-in-law in ten years."

Massa's expression and slight shake of his head told Rebekah.

"Oh, I'm so sorry for your loss." She bowed and touched his robe.

The men settled, performed a ritual hand washing, and made their prayers. As they ate, they told of Ishmael's passing and of the fortunes of his many children, Massa's siblings, with their many wives and large clans. Massa presented Rebekah a gift of a gem necklace, and to Jacob a bronze knife.

"We come on another matter as well." Indicating his son, Massa said, "Daveed is putting together a record of the family, like a tree with all its branches. Isaac has no children besides the twins? I hope I'm not touching on a tender subject, but any other wives or concubines?"

Rebekah smiled smugly. "I've kept my husband satisfied."

"Only the two sons then." Massa wiped the olive juice off his beard with a rag he'd pulled from his shoulder bag. "I understand Esau is the older, so will inherit the farm?"

Jacob spoke up, "That's not necessarily true."

"Esau has married into the Hittite clan," Rebekah explained. "He has land with the Seirs and generally lives with his wife and child. He drops by to see his father every day or two. I wouldn't be surprised to see him here this afternoon."

Daveed pulled from his sack a papyrus scroll and quill pen. He checked with Rebekah for name pronunciations as he wrote, including Adah and Eliphaz. Looking over at his father, he said, "Seems like that's all we need. Will we be moving on?"

"You must stay a few days!" Rebekah insisted. "We get so little company. Perhaps Esau will bring us some fresh meat. If not, we'll slaughter a sheep and have a great feast! We have some Persian wine bought from a traveler saved for just this type of occasion."

Massa nodded his appreciation. "We will rest here for the night. Please understand we have many more families to whom we must deliver our news."

Rebekah went to the stream and refilled the pitcher. Returning, she filled everyone's cups as she studied their faces. *Massa is so handsome and clearly well off. Besides Daveed, he's already mentioned four other sons and nearly as many daughters, I wonder how many children he has?* Glancing over at Jacob she thought of how different life could have been for her. *Is my near barrenness my fault? Have I offended Yahweh in some way?*

"Please relax by the stream," she said, setting the pitcher on the table. "I'll let Isaac know you have arrived and have Kaymah set up a tent for your stay."

"Your husband is well?"

Rebekah dropped her face and Jacob answered. "My father has gone blind and taken to his bed."

"I'm grieved for you." Massa waved a circle of protection in front of him and his son. "Please tell him I will see him this afternoon."

Rebekah left the men in Jacob's charge and journeyed up to the house. She found Esau waiting for her there.

"Whose camels are those?" he demanded. "I checked with Father and he had no idea."

Rebekah began walking past him, ignoring him, but he grabbed her arm. She tried to shake him off, but he held tight.

"Answer me, Woman."

She glared at him. "I'm NOT Woman. I'm your mother, though what I did to deserve such as you, only Yahweh knows."

Esau spat, only missing her foot because she jerked it out of the way. "I asked you a question, Mother. Whose camels?" He tightened his grip on her arm and watched as she tried to hide her pain. He gave it one extra squeeze before letting go.

"We have guests," Rebekah said, rubbing the red mark he'd left on her arm. "Jacob is down with them at the garden arbor."

Esau peered in the direction, though he knew the area was hidden by trees. "Who?"

"Massa and Daveed, Ishmael's son and grandson. They came to tell us of Ishmael's death."

His face fell. "Ishmael died? He was my favorite uncle, out of the seven of Abraham's sons. You did invite them to stay for dinner, didn't you? I'd love to hear family news."

"Of course." She turned her back on him and strode into Isaac's hut where she found him sleeping on his mats, the smell of him heavy in the closed room. Walking across to the windows, she threw open the shutters. The light fell on his face, but he didn't stir.

Kaymah peeked in from the front door. "Shalom?"

Rebekah studied her maid. The old woman was nearly as useless as Isaac, but even an old maid was better than no maid at all. She thought back to the day when Abraham's servant had come to find a mate for Isaac. *I was thrilled by the offer of having my own home, and to marry a man as devout as the servant described. We left the very next day, ignoring my brothers' warnings to give it further consideration. Oh, how impulsive is a girl of fourteen summers!*

"Where have you been?" Rebekah demanded. "Isaac has soiled himself and the room was closed up like a crypt."

Kaymah hung her head at the reproach. "Sorry, Mistress. Your husband, now, he wanted a nap, he did. So your servant, she closed up the windows. Being good, I be, Mistress. Your servant will clean up Master right away. If it so please you, Mistress."

"Yes. And when you've finished that, get one of the shepherds to help you clean the grain hut and put out fresh straw. Ishmael's son and grandson have arrived for a visit. Be sure we have enough firewood and draw some extra water to the cooking hut. Oh, and pull a jug of wine from the barrel and set it up with cups on the feast table."

Rebekah walked down the path to her own hut, next door. Inside she stripped and sponged fresh from the tub Kaymah had set out for her. Slipping into her white dress, she wove some fresh flower stems into her hair before returning to her husband's abode. Kaymah was coming out with the soiled clothes and straw.

Kaymah had left Isaac propped up in a corner, a fresh mat upon his straw bed. With the room lit by the afternoon sun, his face looked particularly gaunt. White clouds floated where his eyes once had been black.

She knelt by his side and stroked his forehead. "Husband, I am here."

His face softened, lips curling upward. Reaching up he took her hand and brought it to his lips for a kiss. "Welcome, my wife. I have missed you."

Settling on her haunches next to him, she took his hand in hers, gently rubbing her finger along the palm, watching him smile at the feel of the familiar gesture. "And I, you, my love," she said. "We have guests."

"Esau told me he saw camels. Who has come?"

"Ishmael's son Massa, and his son Daveed."

"I will greet them." He struggled to pull up against the wall. She stood and tried to help, pulling up under his armpits until he hunched, leaning against the cool clay coated walls. His breath came hard from the efforts, followed by a raspy cough. He seemed to be favoring his right leg, which had a bluish discoloration. With a shudder he settled back onto the ground. Rebekah heart ached for this man once so strong, always so proud, now reduced to soiling himself, too weak even to stand for guests. Could the end be much longer?

"I'm certain they will honor you by coming to your bed, my husband."

Leaving him to rest, she closed the hut's door behind her and found Esau walking into the compound, his arms interlocked with Massa on the left and Daveed on the right. Apparently he was just finishing up some tale or other, for the three of them broke into peals of laughter. Spotting Rebekah, Massa came up and pulled her into a hug.

"Ah, my cousin. You are blessed to have such a fine son as this! A great storyteller, as well as a good provider. He promises to catch us a fine beast for dinner!"

Rebekah remained stiffened in his embrace, glaring instead at Esau who gave her a smug smile. "Yes," she said. "He's quite a man."

Massa let loose and gave the compound a survey. She watched him count the buildings, it took him merely a moment. She wondered how many were in his complex. *Dozens*?

"Where is Isaac?" he asked. "I will speak with him."

Rebekah bowed and pointed. "The hut I've just left. I will bring you in." As she stepped forward the three began following her. She turned back and pointed at Esau. "You were not invited."

"Not for you to say, Mother." Esau jutted out his chin, but she stood her ground.

"The guests are here to speak with Isaac. You must honor their wishes."

Esau's retort was arrested with Massa's light touch to his arm. "If you don't mind, my cousin, perhaps you can join us later. I would rather deliver the news of his brother's death in my own way. I will speak with my uncle alone, but afterwards I'm certain he'll want to see you."

Esau nodded and grasped wrists with each of the men, pointedly ignoring his mother. "As you say. After I have spoken with my father I will go on a hunt, perhaps a gazelle – they have the tastiest meat in the land. Daveed, would you like to come hunting?"

The boy looked to Massa. "May I, Father?"

"Not this time, Son. I will need your scribe skills in just a bit. Please retrieve our bags from the camels and place them where Rebekah shows you."

Rebekah cupped her hands and called, "Kaymah!"

The servant looked out from one of the huts. "Yes, Mistress?"

"Did you tell the shepherd to clean the grain hut as I told you?" she demanded.

The old woman hung her head. "Not yet, Mistress. I be getting the water you be asking. I go now."

Rebekah turned to Daveed, indicating the old servant. "Perhaps you can help Kaymah, Daveed?" With a snap of her head, she indicated Massa. "Come along, Cousin. I will take you to my husband."

Chapter Three: Genesis 27: 1-4

"I am here, Father."

Esau placed his hand on his father's shoulder and smiled as the old man reached up and stroked Esau on his fur spot. The strange red coloration covered the whole back of his right hand, a field fertile with hair so thick it felt like an animal. It had never bothered Esau, and in general people liked looking at it. Adah particularly enjoyed having him rub his fur on her breasts. It seemed only Rebekah had ever considered it an evil sign.

"Esau, my son, I am old."

"Yes, Father." Esau settled against the wall. He studied his father's face, wondering how old he really was. Though he claimed to be considerably over a hundred summers, Esau doubted anyone lived to be that old. He certainly never remembered his father being young, but that was true for all children's memories.

Isaac's blind gaze wandered around the room as he mouthed an unheard prayer. Esau remained respectfully quiet. After a bit, Isaac sighed. "Massa and I have been talking."

"Yes, Father. He told you the news, then?"

Isaac nodded. "Ishmael is dead. Abraham had many more children, but Ishmael was always his favorite. I believe he never forgave Sarah for driving away Ishmael and his mother. You know they almost died in the wilderness?"

"Yes. You've told me that story many times."

"Suppose I have, at that." Isaac let loose of Esau's hand and used both of his to rub his calf.

Esau spotted the muscle spasm and moved to help massage and stretch it. The limb was cold, way too cold. "Does your leg hurt?"

Isaac gave him a wan smile. "I believe I will soon be joining my brother on the other side. Yahweh has sent Massa at the appropriate time. I understand he has brought his son, Daveed, who is a scribe. They are listing my property and I will be dictating my will."

Esau bowed his head. "May your soul be blessed, my father."

"Aren't you curious as to the will?"

"I will honor your wishes, whatever they be."

Isaac laughed. "I knew you'd say that. You're a man of nature. Would you be satisfied if I gave everything to Jacob? After all, he's the farmer. This would be his mother's choice, we both know that, eh?"

Esau took a deep breath, holding it and counting his heart beats. At twenty-seven, one for each of his years, he let it out slowly. "Father, if it will make peace in the family, I will give it all up."

"My son, you are a gem. A true gem. Before I go further, though, I have a favor to ask of you."

"Anything! Just say and I will obey."

Esau came up to take his father's hand again. The old man once more stroked the fur spot, a soft reassuring touch that brought Esau memories of his childhood. *One particular hunt, just the two of us, when we killed a lioness, and Father laid a piece of the fur next to my arm patch, saying he couldn't tell the difference.*

"I would like you to bring Adah and Eliphaz for a visit. How old is he now?" Isaac asked.

"He reaches fourteen summers this year, as old as I was when he was born. Strong and quick, he took down a musk deer last week. Would you like me to bring them to see you tomorrow? I can leave at dawn and fetch them back by high sun."

Isaac nodded. "That would be nice. Perhaps Massa can wait to meet them before he leaves."

"As you wish, Father."

They sat in silence, the flies buzzing around straw not completely cleaned by Kaymah. The sun continued to drop in the sky and Esau began thinking about getting on with his evening hunt. "You said there was one thing you wanted me to do for you?" he prompted. "Was that it; bringing my wife and son to visit?"

Isaac shook his head. "They are good people, even if your Adah loves her perfume and jewelry too much. But they are not of our beliefs, they're Pagan. Esau, my son, you must make me a promise."

Esau waited warily, guessing he knew what was coming.

"I have been speaking with Massa. He tells me he has a sister, Ma'halath. You must go to Massa's homestead and marry this Ma'halath. Her family follows the belief of Yahweh, the God of your father and that of your grandfather. Will you promise me this?"

Esau realized this was to be a condition of his inheritance. Certainly he was happy with Adah, they were very much in love. Still, a man with many wives and many offspring could become wealthy much easier than with only one wife and one son. Already a couple of Adah's uncles had offered Esau some of Adah's cousins as secondary wives, providing he came up with an adequate dowry. That Judith was particularly cute.

In any case, marrying a Hebrew would be a nice gesture towards his father. "Yes, Father. I will go see Ma'halath. If she will have me I will marry her."

Isaac smiled and settled back onto his mat. Esau poured him a fresh cup of water and helped him drink. He returned the pitcher and sat quietly listening to his father breathe. Out the window a songbird serenaded the afternoon air. When the old man again spoke, his voice sounded wistful, the gentle murmuring of a shaded brook.

"Son, I am at the end of my time. Before I die, I fancy a last taste of my favorite dish. I want you to catch a gazelle and spice it just the way I like it, you know how. Bring it to me so I may enjoy this last repast. After eating, I will give you my blessing. Bring your cousins in the tent with you when you bring my meal. They will be our witnesses."

Esau raised his father's hand and kissed it. "Rest comfortably, my father. I do as you bid."

He stopped at the door to gaze once more on the ancient figure. A peaceful glow lit his features, as if his burdens were finally coming to an end. *Was he satisfied with how he'd lived his life?* Esau wondered. *He'd had only one wife and two sons.* Esau vowed his life would be different. More fruitful!

Chapter Four: Genesis 27: 5-13

Rebekah watched her son lope off the property into the surrounding woods. Glancing at the sun, she calculated it as halfway down its arc. It'd be tricky to carry out her plan, a lot of it depended on how long it took Esau to find a suitable gazelle; small and tender. She figured he'd be back just after the sun fell below the hilltop.

"Kaymah!" she called. Receiving no answer she shouted louder, but again without response.

Jacob poked his head out of his hut. "I sent her out to pick some tubers for dinner. What's up?"

"Come here, my son." Rebekah waited in the shade of her hut watching Jacob cross the courtyard towards her. Like his brother he was tall, though in no other way did their appearances match. While Esau's hairy chest held wide strong muscles, this one shone pink and weak. The sun painted the elder a deep copper, but left the younger pale. One dark, one light. One evil, one good.

Jacob came up and knelt before her, taking her hand and kissing it. He rose at her indication, stepped up and walked beside her as she strode towards the sheep pen.

"What do you think of our visitors?" she asked.

She watched him consider. *He's always been this way, thoughtful and prudent; so unlike Esau, who's likely to spout out whatever comes to his mind!* They reached the sheep pen, leaning on it to watch the three calves nurse from their mothers. One ewe let out a contended call.

"They believe in the one true God, Mother. Just before Esau showed up, Massa and I were discussing how the Canaanites worship their false idols, how it blinds them to the wonder of Yahweh's power."

"Your father believes Yahweh sent them with their message of Ishmael's death to remind him to take care of necessary business." She glanced to be sure she had Jacob's attention. He was staring attentively at her, so she continued. "Isaac is about to bestow his inheritance."

Jacob looked across the courtyard to his father's hut. "How do you know this, Mother?"

"I stood outside your father's window and listened. First Massa told of the passing of his father, Ishmael, and then related how the old man had prepared a document describing his wishes for the passing of his possessions. Massa called it a 'will.' He encouraged your father to do one too, tonight, while Daveed is here to record it all. Your father thought it a grand idea."

She paused as a calf came up to them. Jacob reached through the fence rails and petted the baby. "I hope Esau has success on his hunting trip," Jacob said. "I'd hate to have to kill one of our sheep."

"That's exactly what I want to talk to you about. I want you to slaughter one right away and begin preparing a stew for your father."

Jacob looked at her in surprise. "If thus is your command, I will obey. But why not wait for Esau? He usually has a successful hunt."

"I will explain. After Massa left I again stood outside your father's window, this time to listen to his conversation with your brother. Jacob, my son, your father plans to give all that he owns to your brother. We will be left destitute, totally dependent on Esau's whims."

Jacob looked down to his feet, scuffing his sandals in the dirt. Looking back at his mother he shrugged. "Esau prefers to live with the Canaanites. I think he'll just abandon this land to us."

"They're Pagans – idol worshipers." Placing her hand under his chin, she lifted his face to stare into his eyes. "Esau will move his family here, take on other wives, put up alters to their Gods. He'll desecrate our land and leave us outcasts. We need to act quickly, decisively. That birthright is yours, not his. Remember?"

She watched the uncertainty in his face. She appreciated how hard he worked; growing the gourds, tubers, and fruit that sustained them, raising the domesticated animals, and keeping the huts in repair. Surely he'd want to inherit this place?

He kicked the dirt again. "I don't see what I can do. Esau will never tell father he sold me his birthright for a bowl of porridge. Even if he did, Father would never willingly give it to me."

"Then we must get it from him by cunning. You must impersonate Esau and steal your father's blessings."

Jacob laughed. "Father is blind but he's not stupid. He'll recognize my voice, my smell, and my skin."

Rebekah pointed to the lamb he was petting. "Slaughter this one. Make a stew using the spices Esau favors, basil and lavender, without any of your garlic. Cleanse yourself, and dress in Esau's clothes so you smell like him. Wrap the lamb's fur to the back of your hand so when Isaac feels you he'll think you're Esau. I'll have Massa and Daveed standing by to witness once you're ready to secure the blessing. Work quickly, before Esau returns from his hunt."

Her son rubbed the sheep's fur lovingly, looking down into its trusting eyes. The ewe bleated and the lamb broke away, wobbling over. The baby was hardly a month old, a shame to have to sacrifice one so young.

"What if it doesn't work?" Jacob asked. "Father's going to be angry. He'll curse me."

"Let the curse be on me then. In any case, we'll be no worse off than if you don't try." Rebekah bopped him on the back of his head. "Hurry!"

Chapter Five: Genesis 27:14-29

Jacob stood just inside the hut, observing his father. Jacob remembered as a child how active his father had once been, always eager to go off on the hunt, telling stories around the campfire. He'd be up before dawn, toiling until the last few pinks stained the sunset skies.

Jacob squatted on the floor, putting the pot of stew he brought beside him. The family had moved three times before settling on this land of the Canaanites. The happiest he'd been was when they'd been living in Gerar. They'd been rich then, a dozen servants and large herds. He chuckled remembering how Isaac had told everyone that Rebekah was his sister, rather than his wife. When King Abimelech found them having sex he banished them, almost had them all killed.

Isaac stirred, raising his head. "Esau?"

"I am here, Father," Jacob replied, deepening his voice.

His father cocked his head. "Is that you, Esau? I don't recognize your voice."

"Sore throat." Jacob put his hand on his father's chest as he'd seen his brother do. Isaac responded, rubbing the lamb's fur Jacob had placed on his arm. He pulled his son to him in a hug, taking a deep smell of the clothing.

"What have you been rolling in, my boy?"

"Just back from the hunt, Father." Jacob pushed back and, picking up the bowl of stew, placed it in the old man's hands. "Here, my Father. Just as you prefer."

Jacob watched his father's nares widen and face wrinkle as he brought in the aroma. Giving a grunt of satisfaction he raised the bowl and took a tentative sip, smacking his lips. "Delicious. But ... a little different."

Isaac reached in with his fingers, feeling around until he landed on a chunk of the meat which he placed in his mouth, chewing on it slowly. "This doesn't taste quite like gazelle, my son. Is it Kudu?"

Jacob tensed. Was this a trick? "I lucked into a Kudu yearling. Thought you would enjoy this special treat."

Isaac threw the bowl across the room. "You lie!" he shouted. "I know Kudu. This is mutton. Sheep for sure. Are you really my son Esau? Kaymah! KAYMAH!" He shouted repeatedly until the old woman came into the room.

"Calm down, Master," she said, huffing. "You make such racket. My heart, you make it bump-de-bump. What you make this noise for? Look at your mess! Throwing food against the wall! Shamey shame. I as old as you, Master. Why you make me clean up after you all the time? Just 'cause you're blind? Tsk, tsk."

"Shut your driveling, old woman," Isaac called. Pointing in Jacob's direction he asked, "Who is this?"

Jacob raised a finger, shaking it back and forth in front of him. He pointed to the fur on the back of his hand repeatedly and then at himself. "Tell him who I am," he said.

Kaymah nodded. "Why, Master, this be favored son. You no recognize favored son? Tsk tsk. You been lying in bed too long. Brain rotted."

Isaac hung his head momentarily before reaching out and bringing Jacob in for another hug. "Ah, my son, I'm sorry, oh so sorry. Please forgive me. I am old, a foolish old man." Waving to Kaymah he said, "Fetch Massa and Daveed. It is time to give my final blessing."

Jacob pulled away and leaned against the wall, listening to his father tell a story from long ago, some rambling tale which jumped around in confusion of time and place. As the tale wandered, Jacob's own thoughts drifted, thinking about his isolated life on this small patch of land. He had always tried to be a good son, following in the beliefs of his father, honoring both his parents and taking good care of the home. He deserved this inheritance – he needed this inheritance. Esau would be fine with the Hittites.

He looked over to the small alter which Isaac used to make burnt offerings to Yahweh. *What made this different from the Pagan alters*, he wondered. *Was Yahweh watching this drama unfold? Would Yahweh be angry that I'm obtaining my inheritance by subterfuge? There was no understanding of the whims of God. So said all religions.*

Kaymah returned with Massa and Daveed, and Isaac stopped abruptly.

"You wanted to see us?" Massa asked.

"Yes, thank you for coming." Isaac settled back onto his mats. "I wish for you to witness my final blessing. Do you have the document ready?"

Daveed pulled the scroll from his bag and handed it to his father who scanned it. "Yes, just as you told me earlier. It lists all your property; your huts, your land, your sheep, goats, and the small collection of coins and jewelry. All it needs is for you to tell us who is to receive the inheritance and then signatures."

Massa eyed Jacob before saying, "Aren't you going to wait …"

Jacob interrupted him, "There's no reason to wait, is there Father? The hour is growing late."

"No. No need at all. Once more, my son, you must promise in front of these witnesses you will marry into our faith, as we discussed."

Jacob had no idea what he was talking about, but promptly replied, "Yes, Father. As I promised."

"Good, good. Then hear my words, now, in front of Yahweh and these witnesses. All that I own, all my property, all my goods as detailed on the parchment, all of this goes to this, my favored son. Further, all shall be at his will; my wife, her handmaiden, and my other son; and all property rights for eternity. This man is hereby declared my legitimate and only heir, so saith Isaac, son of Abraham. Where be the paper?"

Massa took a small knife and pricked the fingers of both Jacob and Isaac, having each of them make a mark on the paper. He handed the paper over to Daveed and instructed him to take it back to their tent to inscribe the names of all present.

"Why are you not cheering?" Isaac asked. "This is time for a great celebration."

Massa, whose expression had been puzzled since arrival, forced a smile. "So it shall be done. Congratulations Isaac, and to you too, Jay ..."

Once again Jacob interrupted. "Thank you, Cousin. Let us all go outside where we have much to discuss." He kissed his father's hand, stood, and led the others out of the hut.

Chapter Six: Genesis 27:30-40

Esau hung the gazelle leg on the vine at the creek, watching the blood drain from the meat. He thought of how he'd had to leave the rest of the carcass to the jackals and vultures. *Shame.* Fortunately, game remained plentiful, and since he was out hunting by himself the leg was all he could carry back. Walking upstream a few paces, he drank from his cupped hands until sated.

Cutting a few fist-sized chunks off the flank, he rinsed them in the water and grabbed a pot full before climbing up towards the cooking area. Coming out of the trees he took a moment to enjoy the purple streaks on the clouds, glowing above the hills of sunset. Life was good. He enjoyed health, had a beautiful wife and a growing child, and had married into a happy, prosperous community. Enemies were few, and if one could avoid being eaten by a lion or struck by a snake, one could expect to live a long life.

He continued up the hill to the compound as he mused. He hated to see his father dying this way; blind, a bit off his mind, and manipulated by Rebekah. *And this belief in one God, and abhorrence for idols – how could anyone be so sure? The ways of the Hittites seems just fine, their festivals to the Gods of the harvest, the sun, and all the other Gods. Why not? Of course, I'll never tell Isaac about my ambivalence. If he wants me to marry Massa's sister, no problem – as long as she's good looking.*

Reaching the cooking area he took a glowing ember and some kindling, creating the fire he needed for his pot. He chopped the steaks into cubes, adding it to the water and making sure the mixture was heating well before heading to the garden for the tubers and spices he favored. He glanced into the compound as he passed and spotted Massa, Jacob, and Kaymah coming out of his father's hut. Massa looked troubled, though Jacob seemed pleased with himself. He wondered what that was about. *Maybe Isaac asked Massa for another one of his sisters for Jacob?*

Esau brought back the desired plants and threw the spices in the pot to stew. Carving up the tubers and sweet orange roots, he threw them into his pottage for body, adding carrots and turnips for color. Heaped together, the mixture churned in the boiling water, Esau hovering near to enjoy the aromas.

When finally ready, he took the pot off the flames and scooped out a bowl. Up the hill he walked, entering the compound's gate and calling out, "Kaymah!"

She poked her head out of her hut. "What you want, Young Master? Night it is come."

"Bring me a torch. I wish to speak with my father." He waited by the compound gate, counting stars shining brightly in the blackening sky. A waxing half-moon cast eerie shadows across the compound's central courtyard. He stood quietly, the soup held carefully in his hands, listening to the night birds, smelling the breezes, and tasting the evening mists.

Kaymah came holding a long stick with a glowing end held high above her head. "Here."

"No," he directed. "You come with me. I'll want you to witness what Father has to say." He led her to Isaac's hut, and after a respectful knock, led them both inside. He found the old man sleeping.

"Father, I am here."

Isaac startled awake, pushing himself up on one elbow. "Esau? What ... what's happened?"

Esau held the stew under his father's nose wafting the aroma into his face with one hand. "As you bid, I have made your gazelle stew. Do you smell it?"

Isaac took a full whiff. "Ah. Yes! Let me taste." He sat up against the wall, took the bowl in both hands, and swished some into his mouth. "This is it! Yes, my son, it is truly you!" He put the bowl down and grabbed his son, and hugged him tightly. Running his hand down Esau's arm, he came to the birthmark, rubbing it back and forth.

Pushing the boy away he demanded, "If this is you, who was I talking to before?"

"What do you mean, Father? When?"

"Just a bit ago. With Massa and …" His face screwed in agony and he shouted, "KAYMAH!"

The maid, standing just across the room with the torch held up, jumped. "Yes, Master?"

"Kaymah," Isaac demanded. "Who was it I gave my blessing to?"

Her voice trembled as she answered. "As I say, Master. It be your favored son Jacob."

"JACOB!" Isaac grabbed a sandal and threw it in Kaymah's direction. "I knew something was wrong. How could you lie to me like that, Kaymah?"

"I no lie, Master. I say, that be favored son. Rebekah favor that boy. You say you no favor neither. So I figure Jacob be favored, 'cause he favored by one. You see?"

"What … what does this mean?" Esau asked.

Isaac grabbed Esau again, pulling him tightly into a hug. "My boy, my boy. I'm so sorry. I have given all your birthright, yes, everything our family has ever owned, to your brother. You have nothing! Even less than nothing, for I have sworn that you are to be his servant, to do as he bids." With tears crowding his sightless eyes, Isaac turned his head to the ceiling and cried, "Oh Yahweh, forgive me, for I have sinned most gravely."

Esau sat down cross-legged, his head pounding. *How dare Jacob be so cruel as to bring such grief to our father? And for what? A few acres of pasture, a couple dozen animals, and a meaningless right to control?* Despite his anger, he spoke quietly. "Why not call Massa back in and make a new will?"

Isaac shook his head. "I have sealed my word in blood. But that villain mustn't live to benefit from his evil!" Reaching out he waved his hand until Esau came forward and grasped it in both of his. Isaac held tight, stroking the furry spot as he spoke.

"This is my blessing to you. You are obligated to serve Jacob as long as he lives. Therefore you must make an oath to kill Jacob. Let me hear you swear it!"

Esau glanced over at the window and saw his mother, her horrified features flickering in the light of the torch. When she saw Esau staring at her she withdrew.

"Well?" Isaac demanded.

"Father, I love and honor you as much as any son can love their father. Let us not act on such impulse. Sleep on it tonight and tomorrow we will talk again."

The old man shook his head. "No. Such evil must not be suffered. You must swear right now to avenge this dishonor. Are you not a man? A hunter? Do you not find joy in killing of animals? What your brother has done tonight makes him no more than a goat – no a snake. Go kill the serpent before it strikes again."

Esau looked out the window again. Stars shone like a crown of jewels, displayed in a tiara across the sky. He wondered, as he had so many times before, how a man could possibly know if there was one God, or many, or none at all. Clearly there was some force of creation, something providing the spark of life.

He considered his father's request. Yes, he did enjoy the hunt, and the taste of the meat. But killing game was not the same as murdering one's brother. He knew the story of Cain and Able. The Gods never forgave such action.

"Father, I can't do it."

"Then you must send your son," Isaac replied. "Your father has been insulted by his son, so you must avenge your father by sending your son to avenge me. Borrow Massa's camel and fetch Eliphaz. I will speak with him tonight!"

Esau hung his head. Eliphaz hated Jacob, there'd been bad blood between them since the beginning. Because he'd been conceived before Esau and Adah had married, whenever Jacob saw Eliphaz he called him a bastard, belittling him at every opportunity. Eliphaz would love to go on such a mission.

With sadness in his heart, Esau murmured, "As you command, my Father, so shall it be."

Chapter Seven: Rashi's Midrash commentary.

Eliphaz's mouth stretched into a satisfied grin, though his eyes remained cold. The sun had shown its face over the pine trees, shadows had shortened, but his uncle still slumbered. Having caught up to him when most vulnerable, Elkphaz considered running his knife across his uncle's neck now, while he slept. *He certainly deserves it.*

Lowering to one knee, Eliphaz placed the other across Jacob's chest, leaned forward, and spit in his face. Jacob startled awake. He tried to scoot back but Eliphaz increased the pressure on his chest, pinning him hard against the ground. Eliphaz danced his knife before Jacob's eyes before laying its sharp edge on his neck.

Jacob stared up at him in horror. "What are you doing?"

Eliphaz laughed, a low chuckle of disdain. "I'm going to kill you."

"But why?"

The nephew looked off to the heavens, just a moment, before crunching forward, pushing the knife harder against Jacob's throat. "Why? You can't think of a single reason why someone would be angry with you? Nothing comes to mind?"

Jacob reached up, trying to grab the knife, but Eliphaz pushed the blade deeper into his throat, drops of blood dripping down its blade. The older man dropped his hands back to the ground.

"Well? Think of anything?"

"So you're an agent for my brother, huh? I might have known he wasn't man enough to face me himself."

"Oh, you're EAGER to die, aren't you?" Eliphaz said, turning his head slightly to spit again, this time just missing Jacob's ear. "Insulting an honorable man like my father? Shame! My father refused to accept Grandfather's command to kill you. I'm here representing your own father – the man who provided the seed that created your very body. Oh, how cruelly hast thou repaid that act."

"I'm having trouble breathing with your knee pressing against my chest."

Eliphaz laughed again. "Don't worry, it won't be for long."

Tears formed on Jacob's eyes. "You ... you're really going to kill me?"

"Yep."

"Why not rob me instead? Think about it, Eliphaz. My crime was to rob my brother. An appropriate punishment would be to rob me."

"You took everything he had!" Eliphaz shouted, his mouth just inches from Jacob's ear.

"No. I didn't take his life."

Eliphaz thought about his oath to his grandfather. He liked the old man, Isaac had always been kind to Eliphaz. Of course, now he was just a senile old fool. Going through with this murder would prove nothing, and might anger the Gods.

Noticing the hesitation, Jacob spoke eagerly. "I'll give it all back, everything. Just let me live. Didn't Abraham say, 'A poor person is as good as dead'?"

Eliphaz examined his uncle's rounded eyes and blanched lips. What a pathetic fool. "Maybe we could work something out. You swear you'll give up everything?"

"Yes! Yes! Anything you say, my cherished nephew; my dear own flesh and blood."

"Perfect, we'll start with that. If ever you refer to me or my mother again, it must always be in terms of honor. Do you swear? I must hear you swear!"

"Yes! Yes! You and Adah will forever be dear to my heart. I swear!"

"Next. You give up everything you own, understand? Everything in your possession. All claims to any of Isaac's estate. The very birthright you stole from my father. Any claim that my father is subservient to you in any way. Everything, absolutely everything, is now Esau's. Now and forever. You understand?"

Jacob hesitated and Eliphaz twisted the knife, increasing the blood flow.

"YES! On my honor, I so swear."

"Bah, I have no faith in your honor. You'll have to do better than that."

"I swear on my soul, to my very pact with Yahweh, so do I now renounce all claims to everything I own, to any claim on my father's estate, and to my very birthright. Will that satisfy you?"

"Bend one leg up here," Eliphaz commanded. Jacob complied, his bent knee pressed near to his chest. The boy grabbed his uncle's foot and, with a quick slice, removed the little toe.

Jacob howled in pain, grabbing some nearby moss and holding it against the bleed. "What was that for?"

"I'm bringing it back to your father as a souvenir. Besides, it will slow you down just in case you had any stupid thoughts of trying to follow me back." Under the watchful eye of his nephew, Jacob straightened.

"Remove all your clothes," Eliphaz demanded. "Put them in a pile at your feet and then go sit on that log over there."

"You're going to leave me naked?"

Eliphaz took a step towards him, his knife in readiness. Jacob stepped back quickly. "Okay then. My clothes." He removed his tunic and loincloth and set them a foot away. Following the direction of the knife, he crossed to the log and settled onto it.

Eliphaz rolled up Jacob's clothes inside the man's bedpack. Placing the assembly on his own back, Eliphaz threw his uncle a wave and strolled off whistling.

Chapter Eight: Interlude.

Esau studied his mother, staring out to the east as she rested by the large tree stump. In the half dozen years since her husband's death, Rebekah had aged considerably. Her hair, once raven black, had turned the gray of a dead campfire, as dampened as her spirit. At times she talked of returning to her brother, Laban's, home, or perhaps of seeking out Jacob and living with him. But mostly she took long walks alone across the moors. Esau worried she would become lost, or fall and break a bone and not be found, or perhaps be attacked by wild animals.

In the light of the half-waxing moon, just as the sun dipped behind the trees behind them, he brought out a pot of herbal tea with two cups. She glanced at him, but didn't smile or otherwise acknowledge his presence. He placed the cup on the tree stump beside her and settled down next to it.

The crickets began their evening solicitations, songbirds and frogs joining in. Esau scanned the land, dozens of acres cultivated by his clan. It'd be another good harvest this autumn, the wheat was tall and strong, the tubers sprouting well, and the fruit trees ripe with green promise. He looked again at his mother, her mouth curled downward, her brows heavy.

"Mother, why are you so unhappy? Has life truly been that awful?"

She dropped her face into her hands. "My whole life played out as foretold. Never destined for happiness. One good. One evil. So it was foretold." She began crying.

Esau waited for her to calm, sipping his tea and studying the early stars. In the west the sun had sunk, leaving only a few streaks of red in the deepening darkness of heaven. When his mother's sobs had subsided, he murmured, "Please tell me the story, Mother."

"I have never told anyone." Her voice moaned like wind ruffling the tent flaps. "When I was a child of twelve I visited a prophet, an old soothsayer. She gave me a prediction, a terrible fate. At the time I scoffed, but every word has come true. She told me I'd have twin sons, one dark, the other light."

Esau stood and took the other cup of tea to her, placing it in her hands. She didn't glance up at him, but did sip the tea. He noticed how thin she'd become, hardly skin over skeleton. She wasn't as old as Isaac had been at his death, but it looked like she'd given up on life.

"Well, Mother," he observed, "that doesn't seem like such an awful prediction."

"There was more."

He waited, standing above her. When she didn't continue he knelt beside her and lifted up her chin to look in her eyes. They'd become glassy over the years, her face ravaged by too much sun, her teeth old and rotten. "Go on."

"She said one would be evil, and one good. You understand? One dark, one light; one evil, one good. The dark one is you."

Esau stood again and turned from her, pacing back and forth as he considered. He didn't put much stock in soothsayers, but clearly this one had some type of inner sight. He knelt again before Rebekah and asked, "Tell me exactly what she said, to the best of your memory."

She closed her eyes, squeezed them tight. "I remember exactly. She said 'I see two sons. Twins. One will be dark, one light. One evil, one good. Both will found mighty nations, which will forever be at war.' So, you see, I always knew you'd be evil. That is why I favored Jacob over you. And now he's gone and left me with the evil one."

Esau asked, "Did she say the dark one would be the evil one?"

He thought she hadn't heard him, for she hardly moved. He watched her breathe slowly, in and out, her eyes squeezed shut, tears flowing gently. She sat up, and reached for him, grabbing him a deep hug. "Oh, Dear Lord," she whispered. "All these years ... I misunderstood."

Chapter Nine: Genesis 32

Esau hugged his son, delighted with the weight of the bag of coins Eliphaz handed him. "You did well in the market, I see."

Eliphaz nodded. "Yes. The linens your daughters weave have grown quite a reputation. People were bidding higher than ever on the pieces I brought for sale. And the sheep! Yam, the God of Animals, has blessed us with the plumpest, most succulent creatures."

Esau settled at his table, pouring out the coins and sorting them by size and nationality. "So many different types! Moabian. Canaanite of course. And look, a couple of Egyptian gold pieces. You've done very well indeed." He glanced up at his son and noted his frown. "What is it, Eliphaz?"

"Father, I bring worrisome gossip from the marketplace."

"What have you heard, my son?"

"It is said your brother is coming."

Esau felt his pulse pound. Pushing back in the chair, he demanded, "Tell me everything."

"I met a man just in from Paddan-aram down in the market. He says Laban's son, Bethel, finally kicked Jacob and his family off his lands. Jacob's heading this way."

"You're sure of this?"

Eliphaz nodded. Leaning onto the table he drew his face close in to his father's, urgency in his voice. "We must raise an army and kill him. Oh, how I rue the day I didn't run him through when I had the chance. That entire family is evil. The Paddan man said those boys are so bad, they sold their own brother into Egyptian slavery. We must wipe them out!"

Esau returned his attention to the table, fingering the coins, moving them between stacks as if he were counting, though his mind dwelt in the past. *Jacob, oh Jacob. How did you turn out so badly? Must it be as the soothsayer predicted, two nations always to be at each other's throats?* He looked up at his son, now a grandfather himself.

"There's no reason to fight. Let him come. We have plenty of land. If we join families we can remake the clan of Isaac, a greater and stronger people."

"You have always been too willing to forgive, my father." Eliphaz paced to the window and stared out at the fields. He turned back with grim expression. "I beg you to heed my warnings. My uncle and cousins are unscrupulous. They do not come to share, but rather to conquer. Unless we meet them with strength they will murder us and steal all we own." He pointed to the coins on the table. "This money must be used to hire mercenaries. With your permission, father, I will go throughout the lands of Canaan and recruit. There are many who have heard of Jacob and his evil ways. I beg of you – do not be blind to this danger. Our very existence is in the balance."

Esau took the coins and placed them back into the bag. He held it up, but when Eliphaz reached for it, Esau withdrew it. "You may recruit your fighters as a defense. I will not allow an ambush, nor will I sanction the murder of my brother or his family. Further, I will be in charge of all decisions. Is that understood?"

Eliphaz bowed. "Of course, Father."

Esau relaxed against the tree trunk, listening to his two eldest sons and the other clan leaders discussing the plans for the upcoming battle. The sun hadn't topped the eastern hills, where pink clouds glittered in promise. Morning gnats buzzed the campsite, the occasional moth sizzling as it fluttered too close to the campfire flames.

A boy came up with a basket, handing each man a pomegranate and a baked tuber. They paused in their discussion, letting Esau pronounce a morning prayer of thanks. The discussion resumed, Esau listening as he munched. He spit out some seeds and washed down the fruit with a swig from the community water jug.

"I think we should split into three groups," Reuel suggested. "I'll take fifty men and circle back behind Jacob and his clan. We can keep another fifty men in reserve with Esau back here, and you can lead the other three hundred in a show of force, Eliphaz. That way if Jacob tries to retreat I'll cut him off, and if he tries to slip around you, the force here can hold him until you can pinch him. We'll destroy them no matter what."

Esau shook his head. "No. We'll approach them as one force. I don't want to take a chance on them ambushing a smaller group. If they wish to retreat, let them."

"We don't need to kill them all," Eliphaz said, stroking his beard. "Just Jacob and his twelve sons, oh, eleven now. If any of the other men with him offer resistance, kill them too."

"Do we have to kill them?" Esau pleaded. "They're our kin; my brother and nephews, your uncle and cousins."

"They're coming to kill us," Reuel said. "It's us or them."

The boy who'd brought the fruit came back up the hill. "Excuse me, Uncles. Jacob has sent a messenger with a gift."

Esau looked to where two of the family's men were guarding a frightened boy, maybe of eight years, who held a baby lamb in his arms. Esau signaled for the lad to be brought up. When they approached, the messenger laid the bound lamb at Esau's feet, and then supplicated, his face in the earth. Reuel made to kick him but Esau stopped him with a wave of his hand.

"Get up, Boy. Tell us your name."

Warily the boy raised up on his hands, his legs sprawled behind him. "Mercy, I beg of you, Master Esau. I bring offerings of peace." He pointed to the lamb, who obediently bleated. "Your servant, Jacob, who is your blood brother and my great grandfather, begs you to accept our gift and our desire for friendship."

"I asked your name," Esau repeated, and when the boy kept silent, Reuel gave him a kick, sending him sprawling. Esau scowled at his son who responded by kicking the boy again.

"Your name!" Reuel demanded.

The boy covered his head and shivered, rolled up in a fetal ball in the dirt. Reuel kicked him a third time.

"Stop it," Esau said, walking over and laying his hand on the boy's shoulder. Gently, he lifted the boy to a sitting position. The child's wide eyes were tearing, and he was shaking uncontrollably. He looked up at Reuel who had his knife drawn.

"Please don't kill me," the boy pleaded, cowering against Esau's legs.

Reuel grabbed the boy by the hair, stretching his head back and holding the knife against his throat. "Tell us how many men are coming," he demanded. "How many have swords?"

The boy began whimpering, tried to speak, but couldn't make any words. Esau reached down and pulled the knife back and Reuel pushed the boy to the ground. Reuel pointed at him and muttered, "Useless. Might as well kill him now."

The boy's whimpering increased to sobbing as he cowered against the earth. Esau picked up the water jug and brought it over to the boy. Grabbing the boy's arm and pulling him to a sitting position he poured some of the water over the boy's head and put the jug in his hands. "Drink." The boy stared at it with incomprehension.

"Drink. We're not going to kill you."

Tentatively the boy sipped the water as he watched Esau.

"We can't let him go back," Eliphaz said. "He's seen our forces."

Esau watched the boy cower. He had light skin and blue eyes like Jacob, slight build, and even Jacob's nose. *How strange to be at war with your brother's family, and the first casualty to be an innocent child.* He helped the boy to his feet.

"Take your lamb and go back to your family. Tell them all you've seen. Tell them we have a force of over four hundred men. If Jacob wants peace, he can come himself."

The boy nodded, indicating he understood, picked up the lamb, and hurried back down the hill. The three men watched him go past the guards and down the road.

Reuel snorted. "I see your point, but I still say we should have killed him. He's a descendent of Jacob, and that means nothing but trouble."

"The sins of the father shall be passed on to all generations?" Esau asked. "Is that what you believe?"

Reuel shrugged, turning to Eliphaz. Eliphaz, still looking in the direction the boy was scurrying, said, "I swore an oath to Grandfather to kill Jacob. I let him get away once. I shalln't repeat that error."

*****

With the sun arced a third of the way up the sky, the four hundred spread out across the savannah in family clans, groups of ten to twenty men spaced a few dozen strides apart. The woods were thin here, a clasp of trees scattered amidst the ankle high grasses. A scout came up to Esau and his brothers, bowing his respect.

"Shalom, Samuel," Esau greeted. "Report."

Samuel pointed behind him, in the direction the force was moving. "Two leagues ahead, over a second hilltop, await a trio of Jacob's men. They have brought herds of animals. I would think they mean to give these as peace offerings."

"What do you mean, herds?" Eliphaz asked.

"Looks like hundreds of goats, sheep, camels, and cows. Even some donkeys."

"They're going to try to slow us down by loading us up with all that booty," Reuel said. "It's bound to be a ploy. We'll weaken our forces with all those animals."

"Three men? Was Jacob among them?" Esau asked.

Samuel shrugged. "I did not get close enough. You wish me to go greet them and inquire?"

"No, you may rejoin your clan. We'll approach in force."

Esau led the forces forward and as Samuel had said, over the second hilltop they came upon the trio and the substantial menagerie. Here the land stretched out into a great river basin, a natural enclosure for these herds, grazing peacefully on the golden grasses and drinking from the generous creek meandering through the middle. Up the bank of the far side stretched the beginning of woods, perhaps a forest. Three men stood at its edge, dressed in the Hebrew white robes. The middle one, whose shoulder length hair shone black in the sun, waved his arm in their direction.

"I don't like it," Reuel said. "Looks like a trap. They could have a hundred men in those woods, ready to pelt us with rocks."

Esau asked, "Is one of those men my brother?"

Eliphaz shaded his eyes, staring across the field. "None look nearly old enough. I'll send someone." He waved at a group of men standing a few strides away and four came up to them. "Go find out who's up there," he instructed.

"Don't think that'll be necessary," one of them replied, pointing up the hill. "They're coming down."

Esau and his group waited, the men with him shifting nervously. Reuel pulled out his knife and ran a strip of leather along the edge, shining the metal.

"Put that away," Esau hissed, and Reuel stuck it back into his belt.

The three visitors made their way through the animals and waded the stream, climbing back up to within a dozen strides of Esau. The leader, a man of about forty summers, stepped forward and bowed deeply. The other two, who carried bags, kneeled behind him. Esau started to approach them but Eliphaz took him by the arm and whispered, "Let me go – just in case."

Esau shook his head. "I am the head of this family." He proceeded towards the three before him.

Eliphaz signaled to a couple of his own men and with Reuel they all approached the kneeling men. Esau stopped a couple of paces away from them and said, "Rise and speak."

The lead man stood and genuflected. "I am Simone, son of Jacob. We come in peace." Indicating behind him, he said, "My father offers these animals, these servants, and these gifts." He indicated for the man on the left to stand and step up. Reaching into the man's bag, Simone withdrew an intricately casted goblet and a necklace woven of fine stones. He held them out for Esau, but Esau ignored them.

"Why are you here and not Jacob? Is he ill?"

Simone placed the gifts back in the bag as he eyed the men before him. Reuel had taken his knife out and was casually playing with it, running it along his arm and tossing it from hand to hand.

"You terrified the boy we sent earlier. He said you almost killed him. He claimed you had a huge army and were planning on slaughtering us all." Simone looked up the hill at the hundreds of men who had gathered in groups, pointing at him and talking. His gaze then wandered back to Reuel, watching the knife tricks. "My father sent me to find out your intentions."

"My intention," Esau said, "is to speak with my brother. I do not want your servants. I do not want your animals or your gifts. I do not want to speak with you." Esau paused to look up at the sky. Though not yet noon, the heat of the summer lay heavy upon them. "We will rest here for a bit, refreshing in yonder stream. Return now to your father and advise him we will be pressing on. I expect we shall meet up with him before evening. Tell him the only gift I wish to receive is his supplication at my feet."

Simone stood still, his face grim. "Do you intend to kill us, then?"

Reuel stepped forward. "I say kill them all. Let's start with these three so they won't warn their kinsfolk to prepare and ambush us down the road. Letting him go back to warm Jacob of our numbers is foolishness."

Simone's two servants cowered; one of them wringing his hands. Simone stood still. "Is that your intention?" he asked Esau.

Esau merely pointed in the direction Simone had come. "My intention is to speak with my brother. Go now, and tell him to prepare."

Simone stood a moment more, studying Esau's face, and then the other men's. Bowing, he turned his back on the group and, signaling his servants, returned the way he had come.

After a break for refreshments, Esau continued down the road, Eliphaz by his side. Reuel had been sent towards the back of the group to keep order.

"Why do you think Jacob is bringing his family this way?" Eliphaz asked his father.

"Something must have happened with Laban. I guess either Jacob did something that irritated him or perhaps Jacob's family grew too large for the land they had in allotment."

"Surely he knows he won't be welcome here; after the way he betrayed his father, tricking him in the most cowardly fashion. Even if you won't kill him, I certainly intend to."

Esau pointed to a covey of vultures chewing on the bones of a dead cattle just off the path. "Don't be so eager to deliver death, my son. Jacob gained nothing from his subterfuge. Instead of killing them all, let them join us. Our land is rich. We could use the extra herders. If we join the two clans we will make a mighty nation, as Isaac had predicted we would be."

"He is not to be trusted," Eliphaz insisted. "If we accept them into our camp we would have to constantly post guards, else they murder us all in our sleep."

"Surely he wouldn't kill his own brother."

"Able had a brother too."

They came up over a hilltop where the road dipped down into a tree-lined stream bed. On this side of the creek stood five men, white and blue robes bright in the sunshine. Esau recognized one as Simone. Three of the four others appeared to be his age, and the final an older man, gray haired. Esau knew at once it was Jacob.

They stood staring at each other, behind them Esau's men topping the hill and forming a long line, four to six men deep, eighty across. A hawk circled above, watching the gathering of humans with a passive curiosity. Back behind Jacob's crew, Esau could hear the sound of children playing, deducing their camp must be just beyond.

Simone and one of his brothers started to walk forward, but Jacob held them back, raising one arm as a signal. Esau watched him take a step forward, slowly, leaning on his walking stick and limping slightly. Within a few steps he dropped to the ground in a bow. Esau said nothing and Jacob rose, stepped some more, and repeated the dropping maneuver. Still Esau maintained his silence. Seven times did Jacob supplicate, the last one within twenty yards of Esau, where Jacob dropped his stick, letting it lie in the dirt. From there he crawled to within spitting distance of his brother.

Without looking up he pleaded, "Esau, my brother, have mercy."

Eliphaz stepped forward and put his foot on Jacob's back, pushing him flat to the ground. "I swore to your father I would kill you," Eliphaz said. He pulled out his knife, and, holding it up, looked to his father for permission to strike the blow.

The sun, just past its zenith, beat down on the group. Esau studied his brother as he lay still, resigned to his fate. "What say you, Achi?" Esau called.

Jacob coughed, his face in the dust.

"Let him up," Esau said to Eliphaz. The young man glared at his uncle before stepping off. Jacob reached up his hand but instead of helping him up, Eliphaz spit on him. Jacob pushed himself up to a kneel, his face twisted up towards Eliphaz.

"Why would you kill me?" Jacob asked. "I've gained nothing from my father's will. You kept the land, you kept the animals … I entered Laban's land with not even clothes on my back."

"You ridiculed your father," Eliphaz said. "You have come here without our permission with intention of taking back what you wrongly think is yours. If we hadn't brought an army with us, you would be at our throats at this moment."

"No, no," Jacob insisted. "We come in peace. We can remake our families, become stronger."

Reuel stepped up, drawing his knife. "Too much talk. Let's end this now."

Jacob scrambled back a few steps, raising his hands in front of his face. "No, no, I beg you."

Reuel grabbed Jacob by the hair, bending back his head and exposing his neck. He held his knife against his uncle's neck. "Father, just give me the word. First Jacob, then his miserable family."

"NO, NO." Jacob pleaded. "Kill me if you must, but spare my family."

Silence settled on the field, broken only by Jacob's sobs. Esau stepped up to his sons and reached out his hand. Reuel passed him his knife. Esau raised it above Jacob, the sun glittering off its blade. He lowered it slowly until it rested next to Jacob's chest. Then he dropped it to the ground. He reached out both hands and grabbed Jacob around the neck hugging him.

"You are my brother. I welcome you and your family to join us in your homelands."

Simone and his brothers let out a whoop. Esau's army on the hill cheered as well. Eliphaz and Reuel looked at each other and shook their heads.

Eliphaz sent home almost all the men, keeping only a chosen three dozen with him. Jacob ordered a great feast, with the slaughter of twenty goats. Fish were netted from the stream and fresh fruit and berries harvested from the local flora. In the evening light campfires brought warmth as Jacob introduced each of his family.

"You'll stay the night," he urged. "You may have my tent."

Eliphaz poked Esau in the ribs. "No. We best be getting back," he said.

"But it's late," Jacob insisted. "You may get lost."

Eliphaz placed his extended palm flat against his uncle's chest, giving him a little shove. "We'll be safer in the woods than in this camp. Father, it's time to go."

Esau gave Jacob a goodbye hug. "I think it best if we return to our home and family. Our women will be missing us and the livestock need caring. You will come tomorrow, then? We'll leave you a guide."

"Oh, a guide won't be necessary," Jacob said, clasping his brother with both arms. "We'll have no trouble following your path. It'll take us a few hours in the morning to strike camp, and with so mnay animals to herd, it might takes us a few days. Perhaps you can pick us a bit of land?"

"We shall give you a fertile piece, a good spot for you and your family to prosper." Esau turned to the group around the campfire and gave a loud whistle. The crowd grew attentive. "It's time to go. Give your goodbyes and we'll head out." He turned back to Jacob and gave him a parting hug. "Until your arrival then. We'll have another great feast on your arrival."

"Marvelous!"

"Shalom, my brother."

Esau, his family, and their mercenaries gathered and left the camp, heading back northwest, the way they had come. The failing light made the going difficult, but with Eliphaz leading and Reuel bringing up a rear guard they crossed the first stream and gathered together beyond the first hilltop for a conference.

"What do you think?" Esau asked.

Reuel replied, "We should have killed them when we had the chance."

"I agree," this from Eliphaz. "If they come, we will have to constantly be on our guard. With all his sons, they could easily kill us all. I wouldn't put it past them."

"If they come?" Esau repeated.

Reuel snorted. "They're a bunch of thieves and liars. I bet you a stack of silver pieces they'll turn tail tomorrow. And if they do, good riddance to them."

"Let's find out," Esau said. "Reuel, take three men and hide out in the trees tonight. If they start in our direction you can all run here ahead of them. If, instead, they turn south, send two men to let us know and the other two tail them. When they do settle, send another man back to tell us where. The last of you can spy on them for another ten days, then return with news of how they're doing in their new home."

Reuel hugged his father and brother good-bye and picked his three companions. The rest of the group continued on their journey back to the homestead. The moon shone brightly, and the path was easy. They arrived before midnight, joyfully received by their women and children.

Chapter Ten: Genesis 34

Reuel stretched, the early dew dripping on his hair
and beard. He loosened the vines he'd used to keep him
on the tree branch, rewrapping them around the tree.
Spotting his friends on nearby branches he gave a soft
whistle. They all aroused and together they gathered on
the ground. At the nearby stream they splashed
themselves clean.

"You think they're going to join your family?"
Paeter, one of Reuel's cousins asked.

Reuel looked in the direction of the camp, on the far
side of the trees. "I sure hope not. Let's go find out."

The four men crept from tree to tree until they
reached the edge of the woods surrounding the camp
clearing. A few early stirrers were about, including a
preteen girl carrying two buckets who walked near them
as she made her way to the creek. They kept quiet,
careful to stay out of her way. Reuel signaled his friends
and they all scampered into the treetops where they
could watch both the camp and the brook. A steady
stream of Jacob's clan came and went from the creek.
Cooks fueled the campfires and the smell of porridge
and cooked meat wafted up to Reuel.

He watched Jacob and a handful of his sons huddle
around a campfire in discussion. Reuel strained, but
over the background of morning birds, bleating goats,
and giddy children, he couldn't hear their words. After
they'd finished their breakfasts, Jacob's sons scattered to
the various tents and organized the striking of camp.
Gathered by families they headed out of camp heading
south, the opposite direction from Esau's homesite.
After the last had left, and even before the dust settled,
Reuel climbed down from his perch. Keeping Paeter at
his side, he sent the other two back to Esau to give the
report.

Following Jacob's crew was easy for Reuel and
Paeter; with all the animals and children the large group
made slow progress. They traveled for a week, making

only a few leagues a day, until they reached a fertile valley rich with grain and livestock. A collection of a score of huts sat on a raised knoll, a bucolic scene that reminded Reuel of his home. He recognized this place as Sheshem, the land of Hamor and his sons.

"You know Hamor, don't you?" he asked Paeter.

"Yes, I helped with his planting and harvest for four seasons. He and his son, Shechem, are good men. They're a small family, a dozen men, perhaps thirty residents in all, counting servants and children."

"You think you can sneak into Hamor's compound? You can warn them about Jacob's family's treachery."

Paeter looked out over the fields before him, perhaps a hundred hectacres, where Jacob's crew was settling into a pasture closed off by a stone fence. "I better hurry," he said. "Even if Jacob doesn't send an envoy, Hamor's certainly going to want to know who these squatters are."

"Good." Reuel looked up in the skies, where a few dark clouds were rolling in from the west. "I'll go back and report to father. I should be back in five or six days. See that tree branch there?"

Paeter looked where he pointed and nodded.

"When I return I'll hang a white rag with blue fringe. You be careful, okay?"

They hugged, and Reuel watched his friend backtrack into the woods and begin the circle around the pasture to come in to Hamor's camp from the far side. Once he'd left, Reuel refilled his water sack at the creek before taking off on his journey.

Reuel's trip took the predicted six days, and on his return he climbed the tree he'd designated and hung the marker. Looking out from his perch he surveyed the fields. Jacob's family had set up tents in their pasture and had established pens for their animals and for crops. Laundry hung on strung vines. Cook pots steamed on small campfires. The sounds and smell of livestock rolled in over the green hills.

Spotting a bird's nest, Reuel raided it for its eggs, bringing them down to add them to the remainder of the bread he'd brought from home. Afterwards he set up his hammock in the tree and napped.

He awoke to the shake of his hammock by Paeter, who'd climbed up after him. Reuel extracted himself from the sling and joined his friend on the ground, exchanging hugs. Paeter had brought him fruit and meat from Hamor's town. The two enjoyed their repast as Paeter filled him in on the news.

"It's been a whirlwind six days," Paeter said. "Hamor and Shechem welcomed me with open arms; always have been kind people, though a bit naïve. I tried to warn them of Jacob's history of duplicity, but they were eager to give him the benefit of the doubt. They sold him that land they've camped on for a hundred pieces of silver."

Esau glanced in the direction of the camp, assessing the size and the rich topography. "That doesn't seem like very much for all that land."

"As I said, they're nice people. But wait til you hear what happened next. Seems Jacob's got a daughter, a cute little tart named Dinah. You remember her?"

Reuel tried to recall which of Jacob's offspring she might be. "Was she the girl with the marvelous breasts straining to get out of that red dress?"

Paeter gave him a wink, "Yeah, she does make an impression! So the land purchase was finalized on the second day and that evening there was a big party in celebration. A lot of wine was drunk."

Reuel laughed. "I love a good party."

"Anyway, as I was saying, a lot of people ended up drunk, and in the morning Dinah woke up in Shechem's bed."

"Well, that should have confirmed the business deal, eh?" Reuel took another bite from the mutton chop and a swig from the jug. He smacked his lips in appreciation, six days of almost non-stop running had taken off some pounds.

Paeter's smile faltered. "One would have thought so, but there's been a complication. I suspect Jacob's family planned that whole bit out, telling Dinah to get herself seduced so they could pretend they were outraged. It could have been trouble, but turns out Shechem was a virgin and blown away by his first sexual experience. He thinks he's in love and wants to marry the harlot."

"Really? Heh. I remember my first sex. Talk about a gift from the Gods. Of course, I was fourteen at the time. How old is Shechem?"

"Almost twenty – sort of a mama's boy. In any case, even agreeing to marry Dinah wouldn't satisfy Simone and Levi. They said in order for Shechem to marry Dinah he had to adopt the customs of Abraham … ALL the customs, if you get my meaning."

Reuel shuddered. "Circumcision at that age will be excruciating!"

"It's worse than that. Simone is insisting the whole family go through the ritual. The plan is to have a party tonight where everyone gets drunk and then perform the ceremony on all the males. There are fourteen men, not counting me."

Reuel looked out to the compound. He wondered at the willingness of Hamor and his family to go to such extremes for the sake of harmony. He doubted he'd do such a thing, especially not for a family as corrupt as Jacob's. On the other hand, he might feel he had no choice; cooperate or be at war.

"Are you going to be there?" Reuel asked.

Paeter shook his head. "I'm already cut. I figure I'll sneak out in the middle of the party, before they get to the surgery. I'll hang out here with you tonight and in the morning we can go into town and take care of the family and animals."

That evening Reuel climbed the tree at the edge of the clearing. He could see the bonfire and people dancing and drinking, their laughs and songs echoing across the clearing. Resisting the temptation to join them, he closed his eyes and listened to the tunes, many of them familiar from his youth. The moon rose, arcing a quarter-way up the sky before Paeter joined him, bringing a basket of food and a wine sack.

Reuel ate until he couldn't take another bite, and with the wine, he was just dozing off when he startled awake at the sounds of screaming coming from the compound. He saw Paeter standing and staring in that direction.

"I can't believe they're going through all this at Jacob's insistence," Paeter said. "I bet there's more to this than he's saying."

Reuel came up next to him, and together they stood vigil until all was silent.

The sun had crested above the hills when Reuel opened his eyes the next morning. Paeter had already left, so Reuel wandered down to the stream and made his morning ablutions. He'd almost finished when he heard Paeter calling him.

"Here, down by the creek," Reuel replied.

Paeter rushed through the brambles, emerging through the bushes carrying a girl of about four or five summers in his arms. He set her trembling form on the ground where she grabbed his leg, holding tight. Reuel looked up at his friend's grim expression.

"What?"

"They're dead, all dead," he hissed. Bending, he picked up the young girl again, allowing her to snuggle into his chest. "This one called out to me from her hiding place. She's so traumatized she barely could tell me what happened."

Reuel grabbed a tree for support. "What are you saying?"

Paeter settled onto the ground, and resumed comforting his charge. "Get her some drink," he suggested.

Reuel filled his water sack and brought it to her. Holding the opening to her mouth he let her have her fill while he gently stroked her hair. "What happened?" he asked.

"Bad men." Though she spoke in Canaanite, her accent was heavy. "They kill my mommy and daddy and … everyone." She turned her head back into Paeter's chest, who rubbed her back lovingly.

"This is what I figure from what she's told me," he said. "After Jacob got all the men drunk and did the circumcisions, Hamor's family were, naturally, too weak to defend themselves. Simone and Levi led a couple of the other brothers in a mass murder of Hamor, Schechem, and all of their comrades and servants. They killed every single one; including the women and children, except this one who managed to hide. I ran a rough count of thirty-eight bodies. How could the Gods allow such evil? And Hamor had been so kind and generous."

Reuel bent forward and wiped a tear from the girl's face. She snuggled further into Paeter's chest. He stood, holding her tightly in his arms. "Let's hit the road. I'm eager to bring Sebeth to her new home."

Chapter Eleven: Mishrah commentary

Esau watched his great-grandson repairing the goat pen's fence. He couldn't recall the boy's name, but clearly the young man had a natural talent with rope, binding and knotting in a matter of a few heartbeats, testing for strength, before moving down to the next joint to bind it as well. Esau studied the pen, counting the goats, including five new kids nursing at their mother's teats.

Tiring, he settled onto a large stone, his gaze wandering across the field to the olive grove. There the twenty saplings planted the previous season all showed greenery of productive life. *This is a rich land, a glorious home.* He sighed, trying to shake the weariness that'd settled in his bones over the past year. Age had treated him kindly, but his joints creaked in the mornings, and climbing the holy mountain now challenged his breath.

Turning to the east he saw a figure approaching. His vision was cloudy these days, but not so much he couldn't recognize Eliphaz, now an old man himself. His son limped from a poorly healed hip fracture, but at least he was alive. Esau thought of Reuel's death, how a simple thorn prick had developed into a pus pocket, how the redness had spread up his leg and after only two days of rigors, had left him dead. So many of his family had died, and soon it'd be his turn.

Eliphaz bowed before his father before rising to kiss his hand. "I am here, Father."

"Welcome my son." Esau pulled him into a hug. "What news?"

"I bring word of Uncle Jacob, my father. He has passed."

Esau thought of Jacob as a young man, how religious and sure of himself he'd been. Now he finally would find out if his belief in one God was correct. "We are given only so many years, and Jacob and I have both lived long. Our families have prospered and grown strong. No doubt we'll both have long legacies."

Eliphaz spit and ground it into the earth. "We have prospered honestly, but Jacob's descendants are thieves and bullies."

There had been constant trouble between the two tribes, Esau knew and regretted it. Jacob's family had often sent raiding parties onto Esau's land, stealing animals, and occasionally women. Eliphaz had sent retribution parties back, and though they were currently not fighting, the two families would likely flare into conflict again at any time.

"They're not all evil, and we're not all good," Esau advised. "You must seek compromise and peace. Forgiving is not that hard once you give it a try."

Eliphaz stood and walked over to lean on a goat pen post. His grandson came over and Eliphaz complimented him on his rope work. Turning back to Esau, he said, "I honor your advice, Father. But forgiving involves reformation, and it's clear Jacob's clans haven't learned their lessons."

Esau dropped his gaze. *My time is past. I can only be an observer now.* Looking back up at his son, he asked, "Where will he be buried?"

"His family insists in the Cave of the Patriarchs. It's on our land, and I don't feel he deserves this honor. They are proceeding anyway. To stop them we'd need to raise an army. I've come to seek your counsel."

Esau turned to the north, in the general direction of the cave. It was the family's holiest site, the burial place of Abraham, Sarah, Isaac, and Rebecca. In nearby caves Ishmael and some of his family had been entombed. When he passed, Esau hoped to be buried there as well.

"No, let it be."

Eliphaz bowed his head. "As you command, my father."

Esau lifted his walking stick and sketched a design in the dirt. Pictures of his childhood seemed more frequent these days, squeezing out more recent memories. "I'd like to be present at my brother's funeral," he said.

"Then we should bring an army to protect you."

Esau's thoughts drifted back to the raising of the four hundred. The strategy had worked, forcing Jacob to move to other lands. After hearing about Hamor, Esau had told Eliphaz he had been right. But, surely, this time would be different. "No," he said. "To avoid trouble, perhaps I should go alone."

Eliphaz bent to one knee and took his father's hand, giving it a kiss. "I will accompany you, my father, to the very doors of death." He stood and called to his grandson. "Baleith, come here."

The young man came to the beckon and bowed at his grandfather's feet. Eliphaz touched the boy's head and the teenager rose to give him a hug and a kiss on the cheek.

"It is good to see you, Grandfather."

"And you as well, Baleith. Are there others within calling distance?"

Baleith looked up towards the house. "Most of the men are out in the pastures. Faulkber is resting, recovering from his illness. Many of the women and children are home."

Esau put his hand on Eliphaz's shoulder. "We can travel quicker if there are few of us."

"Very well." Turning to Baleith he asked, "You have a knife?"

Baleith pulled a small one from his belt. "This and a sling shot. Are we going on a raid?"

"We're going to the Cave of Patriarchs," Eliphaz replied. "Your great-uncle Jacob has passed and we are going to attend his funeral."

Baleith bowed. "As you command, Grandfather. Do we leave in the morning?"

Eliphaz glanced at Esau, who replied, "No, we leave now." He turned and began walking north. He didn't look back but could hear the two men talking as they fell in step behind him.

They walked deep into the evening hours, reaching Seir after the sun had set, the waxing moon already up casting shadows, painting the fields in shades of gray. They aroused Hassan, Esau's brother-in-law, the current patriarch of the Seir tribe, and he welcomed Esau and his two family members warmly. He provided them a bit of food and drink, and helped them settle into a community hut.

In the morning Esau awoke with the call from the ubiquitous roosters, the blessing and bane of domesticated peoples. Incessantly announcing their pride, a triumphant predawn cry by one was picked up by the next, followed by cousin after cousin in an obnoxious cacophony of discordant choirs.

Esau halted mid-stretch, as his back and bad hip complained of the excessive walking and lumpy straw palate he'd subjected it to the previous evening. The urge to get up after only a few hours' sleep to empty his bladder overcame his desire to stay in bed, followed by sleeplessness, one of the many curses the Gods subjected on old men.

Around a cooking fire, he found a couple of young women preparing the morning meal for the family compound while Hassan sat on a nearby tree smoking a pipe as he supervised. Esau studied him, Adah's younger brother, the only surviving member of that generation. The years hadn't been unkind to him, a triple chin hung heavily over a generous belly. Laugh lines mapped his face. Esau thought back to their youth, when they used to hunt together. Just two years his junior, they'd been best friends in those days.

He remembered one hunt, deep in the late autumn, with the leaves golden and the wild grasses grown high and wild. The three of them, Esau near thirty, Hassan the two years behind, and Eliphaz, a strapping young man in late teens, brought down a great stag. Just afterwards, Esau and Eliphaz had been ambushed by a den of lionesses; four of them there were. Hassan's prompt attack, with his screams and stones thrown at the beasts, had broken the attack and saved their lives.

"It's been many a season since last we had the honor of your visit," Hassan said, indicating for Esau to sit next to him on the log. "And you bring me the pleasure of the company of your son and great-grandson. Are you on a visit or a pilgrimage?"

Esau settled next to him, accepting the offered pipe and enjoying a draw of the sweet tasting herb smoke. "As it happens, I am on a mission. Eliphaz brought news of Jacob's death. We are traveling to attend his funeral." He took another toke of the pipe, letting the smoke dance gently on his lips and mustache. He felt a calmness permeate his thoughts, and wondered if the pipe's herbs were medicinal. He handed it back to Hassan who held a burning coal to the bowl to reignite the packing, inhaling deeply and holding the smoke long, before letting rings puff out from his nose and mix comradely with the cook-fire smoke.

"Jacob's dead, eh?" Hassan sighed. "Well, one mustn't say evil about the dead. I suppose I can think of something nice to say at his funeral." He took another drag from his pipe, the two sitting in companionable silence watching the women stir the pot of beans. After a bit Hassan said, "Actually, I can't. Can you?"

Esau thought back to the first thirty years when he'd lived with his twin brother. There were so many negatives; the extortion of his birthright for a bowl of porridge, the meanness around the house, the trick he played to their father on his deathbed … the list went on and on. Afterwards, the troubles he caused in Laban and the murder of Hamor and all his family … it was hard to find anything good to say about him. "Well," Esau drawled, "at least he was a good cook."

Hassan snorted. "And apparently a heck of a stud; two wives, two concubines, a dozen sons and at least as many daughters. It just goes to show even the worst scoundrels have SOMETHING good to them."

One of the women brought bowls of beans to Esau and Hassan. She handed one to each and kneeled in front of Hassan, who leaned forward and kissed her forehead. "Off with you, Deboralah," he said. She retreated back to the campfire to dish out more beans. Esau watched the woman's retreat, lithe and supple, her buttocks bouncing beneath her tight frock.

"Where is he to be buried?" Hassan asked.

"The Cave of the Patriarchs. Eliphaz said the funeral's tonight. You want to come?"

Hassan rose and stretched, his back cracking like a green log in the fire. He held out his limbs, one at a time, shaking first the arms and then the legs laughing as he did so. "You think this old body could make that twenty league march? It's been ages since I crossed into Ephron's land."

Esau stood, too, and together they looked east. Esau remembered the last time he'd been to what was then called the cave of Mach-pe'lah. His father's funeral had been a quiet event. Jacob hadn't attended, only Esau and his extended family. "They won't give us trouble for crossing their land, will they?"

"No," the fat man replied. "The Hittites won't be the problem. My worry is how Jacob's clan will treat you. They're a scandalous lot, everyone knows it. If you're going you should take a big force. I'm not up for the trip, but I can loan you a dozen servants armed with clubs and knives."

Esau settled back onto the log and resumed eating his breakfast. His teeth had lasted well for his age, a source of pride, but soft foods like this were easier on them than heavy fruits or gnawing on bones. He settled back and enjoyed the warmth of the sun, just rising over the eastern groves.

He considered Hassan's offer, and whether he wanted to approach the funeral in this fashion. Bring an armed mob to a funeral? Surely his nephews would tolerate an old man coming to give last respect to his brother.

He looked up at Hassan who was waiting for his answer. "Thank you, my brother. But I respectfully decline. It might be best for me to go alone."

After a bit he returned to the tents and awakened Eliphaz and Baleith and told them he planned on continuing the journey alone.

Eliphaz objected strenuously. "They will kill you, Father; they're vicious, particularly Simone and Levi."

Esau placed his hands on his son's shoulders, leaning forward and kissing him on each cheek. "You may be right, and if so, that's even more reason for me to go alone. If they kill me, it'll only be one death."

"I will come," Eliphaz announced.

"I forbid it."

Eliphaz placed his hand on his father's chest. "You may forbid me to accompany you, but you can't stop me from following you. I will stay in hiding once you arrive. If they greet you fondly, then I will join you. If not, well, at least I'll know what happened."

Esau started to object, but could see that Eliphaz's mind was decided, so he shrugged and turned to his great-grandson. "Baleith, stay here with Hassan's family. Hopefully we will both return by tomorrow evening. If neither of us does, you will know that we have been killed."

Baleith bowed. "As you command, so shall I obey."

Esau left them, finding Hassan waiting outside the tent. "I think you are being foolish," the fat man said. Esau placed his hand on the fat man's shoulder and gave him a wink. Without another word he walked past him and down the path to the east.

The sun had reached the western treetops when Esau arrived at the series of caves just east of Mamre. His travel through the land of the Hittites had been easy, with three stops at little farmhouses along the road where the hosts had welcomed him with fresh water and fruit. Twice the landscape had broken so that Esau could look back for a league behind him and both times he spotted Eliphaz following. He was a good boy, always had been. His mistrust and hatred of Jacob's family remained unshakable his whole life.

Just before sunset Esau came upon the river Er, with its long series of caves. Though it'd been twenty years since he'd last visited, he knew exactly which held his family's crypt. As he walked along the riverbank he could hear voices, and turning the bend he found a crowd of a dozen men, all dressed in the blue tinged white robes characteristic of Jacob's clan. He crouched behind a rock watching them.

The group stood with heads bowed, praying above a shroud wrapped body. It made a peaceful scene, and Esau couldn't believe they would turn violent. Nerving himself, he rose and walked towards the group. He had approached within a dozen yards before one man noticed and grabbed another's arm, turning him to see. When this man turned towards him, Esau saw it was Simone.

"Who be you, coming to disturb a family in grief?" Simone demanded.

Esau took another three steps and bent to one knee, bowing before them. Simone came up and touched him on the shoulder. "Rise and be recognized."

Though old now and shortened by age, Esau still stood taller than most men, and at full height was nearly half a hand taller than Simone. He saw recognition dawning in the younger man's eyes.

"Uncle Esau? I ... I can't believe it!"

"Yes, my nephew. I come in peace to share this commemoration of the death of my brother."

Simone took him in a hug, kissing both cheeks. "Welcome my uncle. You may join us in peace."

The group opened up, then closed around him as he joined in their prayers. The sun edged down past the hills, night birds and crickets awakening to add their calls to the dirge of the family. Mosquitos came to feast and Esau slapped a few, leaving spots of blood on the welts they left behind.

"It is time," Levi announced. "Let's get this done and get away from the pestilent insects."

Simone turned to Esau. "Thank you for coming, Uncle. You may have the honor of helping to carry your brother into the Cave of the Patriarchs."

Esau bent down and kissed the shroud covering his brother's head. The putrification of a man three days dead wafted up to greet him and for a moment he staggered. One of the other men held out a hand and he grabbed it, settling to the ground and taking a few breaths.

"Perhaps," Esau said. "Perhaps you would consider burying Jacob in another cave."

The boys looked at each other. "Why would we do that?" one asked.

"Well, there are so many of you. When it comes time for your children to bury you, this cave will be too full. Why not leave it as a special place for Abraham, Sarah, Isaac, and Rebekah? Ishmael is buried in that cave over there." Esau paused to point down the creek. "Perhaps you would like to start a family crypt a bit further down, too?"

Levi glared at him. "You don't think Jacob's good enough to be buried with his father, is that what you're saying?"

Esau brought himself to a stand, and stepped up to his nephew, getting within inches of his face. He could smell the rotten breath coming from the frowning mouth, an ugly orifice in a face pockmarked by years of disease and fighting. The viciousness of Jacob seemed particularly rabid in this man, one who could never be satisfied without trying to cheat his way to something better. On instinct he spit in the boy's face.

Somebody gasped, but the other men all stood silent, astonished. Levi reached up with one sleeve and wiped it off. He turned halfway aside, and Esau took a breath, meaning to apologize. Before he could get a word out, Levi swung back at him, plunging a knife deep into Esau's belly.

Intense pain radiated up to Esau's chest, neck, and into his head. He staggered back, grabbing at the wound with both hands as he collapsed onto the ground. Two of Levi's brothers grabbed him and pulled him back, while Ben, another of the boys, rushed forward.

"NO!" Eliphaz screamed, rushing from his hiding spot. He ran across the opening, pushed Ben aside, and knelt to cradle his father's head in his hands. "Oh, Father, what have they done?"

Ben stood a step away. "I'm sorry, Cousin. This never should have happened."

Eliphaz's tears dropped onto his father's face. Looking up he shook his fist at the group. "I curse you, evil spawn of Jacob. I swear my descendants will forever be your enemies. May you all become slaves of the Egyptians, unto twenty generations. Even afterwards, you will wander homeless, persecuted anywhere you try to reside. Though you will greet all as if you come in peace, you will never find peace. This is the curse I place upon you and all your descendants forever."

The End

Zipporah

Chapter One: Moshe Brings a Guest

Zipporah shaded her eyes, protecting them from the glare of the evening sun on the prairie. From the sound of the dogs' barking, she knew her husband had finally returned. Squinting down the westward path, she could just make out the approaching shadows pass among the olive trees and fields of grazing sheep.

She saw that Moshe came not just with the ass, loaded with goods from the town, but with a stranger as well. *Surely that young man in the ragged white linens is a slave. Has my husband bought a servant at the market? Truly we could use extra help, but another mouth to feed?*

Zipporah rushed out the back of their lodge to the tumbling creek, splashed water on her face and under her arms, and ran back in the home. She slipped into the green reed dress which accented her figure, still trim despite birthing the two children. Moshe had a dozen summers on her, yet still found her desirable most every night. She hung her golden El amulet around her neck. Brushing her hair quickly, she returned to the front door to kneel.

Moshe paused at the door, wiped his feet, murmured a prayer, and delivered a touched kiss to the scroll hung on the doorpost. Zipporah noted with surprise that the slave said the prayer with him.

A Hebrew, she thought. *My husband has brought home a Hebrew slave.*

Moshe entered and placed his hand under Zipporah's chin, tilting her face upwards. He kissed her gently on the forehead. "I am ha ... home, my loving wa ... wife."

Zipporah stood and they embraced. "Welcome home, my honorable husband. I give thanks to the great

God El, for he has guarded you zealously on your journey, yea, even unto our doorstep."

She observed Moshe's sad face with its wrinkled brows and tired eyes. Yet his lips turned up in a quirky smile.

"I … I'm not so sa … sure 'twas El wa … watching," he said. He turned and pointed behind him. "Zipporah, th … this is Amichai."

Zipporah nodded slowly, in what could have been taken as a bow, unsure from the introduction if she was to treat the fellow as a guest or a new servant. Seeing him standing a few feet away outside her tent, she confirmed the impressions she had made from the distance. A handsome youth, perhaps of sixteen summers, his loincloth was of the cheapest cotton, surely Egyptian scraps. Dried mud splattered most of his body; his palms boasted thick calluses. He bowed on one knee and she noted a dozen healed whip marks across his shoulders.

"Yes, my husband. I see him."

Moshe laughed. He spoke something in the harsh Hebrew tongue and the young man stood and smiled nervously. He said something back to Moshe who laughed again.

"My la … loving wife, Amichai wa … will be our ga … guest for a few suns."

"Thank you for your kindness, honorable lady," Amichai said with a heavy accent.

"Oh, you speak Midian," Zipporah said. "Welcome, my guest." She offered her hand and he kissed it.

Ah, Moshe has brought me this wanderer as a gift. What a clever man he is. The fellow will entertain us with marvelous stories for a few days just for the price of food and a new loincloth. Then just as he's getting tiring, off he'll go. Scoot, scoot. Praise be to El for having delivered unto me such a wise husband.

She pointed towards the back of the hut. "Please feel welcome to cleanse yourself in the creek, Amichai. Follow the path you will find from our back door, downstream, where the bushes provide you privacy and peace. We'll bring you some suitable clothing."

"I ga … go put away Per … Pershan." Moshe said, pointing at the loaded ass tied to a palm tree.

Zipporah reached up and pulled him down for a deep kiss. "I am truly glad to see you, Moshe. I see from Pershan's load you have been successful on your bartering trip, as well as bringing this entertaining guest. I'll prepare cabbage rolls for our evening meal. After dinner I will rub your sore muscles with some sweet Assyrian oils."

Kissing his fingers, he touched them to her lips, turned, and repeated the gesture for the little scroll box hung on the doorframe. He walked out to the evening air and Zipporah followed. She cupped her hands to her mouth, and shouted, "Kaleilah."

"Here, Aunt Zippo," a sweet voice replied.

Zipporah spotted Kaleilah standing in the small vegetable patch bordering the creek upstream. Her brown shift flapped above the long deer legs she had been growing the past half year. She rushed up the hill with a basket of onions, bowing before Zipporah.

"Who did Uncle Moshe bring home? Who is that? Is he going to be our new slave? He certainly is good looking, isn't he? What happened to his back? How come he speaks so funny? I could barely hear him from way over there in the garden. What did he say?" In Kaleilah's excitement she spilled the basket she had placed at her feet.

"Oh, Moab moles," she cried, bending down and tossing the onions back into the basket.

Zipporah laughed at the youngster's enthusiasm. "Your honorable uncle has brought home a Hebrew guest. I'll take care of these onions. Please hang a tent for our visitor from the big oak tree and bring a robe and a pair of sandals to our guest at the bathing spot. Where are the boys?"

"They're playing with their cousin Aaridie at his hut, Auntie." Kaleilah pointed in the general direction, across the olive tree grove.

An image of her father's compound a league away came to Zipporah's mind. Unlike this one, that site held a dozen stone structures. Besides her father, four of her siblings' families lived there with a handful of servants. Her two sons loved to play with their cousins, and it was good that they did, to form family and cultural bonds.

"After hanging the tent, go get them so we can prepare for dinner. Tell Gershom to make sure Eliezer washes his hands."

"I will do as you bid." Kaleilah bowed and headed to the storage hut for the tent.

Chapter Two: Telling Tales

Kaleilah stirred the delicacies placed before Amichai with her finger. Deftly she grasped a plump olive between her thumb and forefinger, dipped it in the mustard sauce, and placed it on his outstretched tongue. He let it sit there a moment, the succulent juices dribbling down his throat.

"You la ... like sweet Hur ... Hurrian olives?" Moshe asked him.

Amichai nodded vigorously. "First time I've ever had such a treat. They're great! Until I escaped from Egypt a fortnight ago, I'd only had slave food. I humbly bow to your great graciousness, Lady. I praise Yahweh, who has brought me to the promised land of milk and honey."

Zipporah tutted. "Yahweh is not the God of this home, Amichai. El rules these lands, and it is only to El and his children that we worship here."

Amichai looked at Moshe, and back at Zipporah. He bowed his head. "My apologies, honorable lady. I had assumed since this was the home of The Great Moshe, Yahweh would rule supreme."

Zipporah lifted an eyebrow at Moshe. "So, it's 'The Great Moshe,' is it? Perhaps there is more to your inviting this guest than I first thought." She turned back to Amichai. "Do tell me more of this story, my guest. Why do you refer to my husband in this way?" She signaled Kaleilah to refill Amichai's wine glass, from which he took a deep draught.

Moshe indicated for the girl to bring Amichai more bread as well.

Amichai clearly was enjoying himself. Zipporah guessed it probably was the first meal he hadn't had to beg or steal since he escaped.

"Everyone's heard of 'The Great Moshe,'" Amichai said to Zipporah. "Like I told him by the long oasis, your husband is a legend to his people. The story of how he slew the evil taskmaster Phillius is told and retold around the campfires. Phillius was a giant, the legend goes, seven and a half stone high. His strength was that of an oxen, his muscles hard as tree trunks. Phillius murdered dozens of Hebrews, for the littlest or no offense, whipping them to bloody corpses in front of all their friends, and gloating."

Amichai stood, turned his face to the heavens, shaking his fists. Then he sat again and smiled. "Ah. The Great Moshe stood up to him; Moshe, the Princess' stepchild, and honored Hebrew of the Pharaoh's court. They battled mightily, with blows by the giant thwarted with counterblows by the Prince. The people watched in awe, the story goes, and Yahweh stepped in on his son's behalf. The end came quickly, lightning guided by the hand of Moshe struck Phillius right between the eyes, smote the giant, who crashed like the falling of a huge tree."

Amichai paused to savor another olive placed in his mouth by Kaleilah before continuing.

"There were rumors you had settled in Midian, Moshe. When I escaped, naturally I came here to see. And, oh, beyond my wildest expectations, I find all to be true. I have been delivered from bondage, just as the prophets say will happen to all of our people. Praise to Yah ... oh, excuse me. Well, praise to God, anyway," Amichai finished sheepishly.

Kaleilah looked at Moshe in awe. "Really, Uncle Moshe? Is that really how this happened? Your God must truly be a marvelous God to have such ..."

"Kali! Watch your tongue."

Biting her lip, Kaleilah turned to Zipporah. "Oh! I didn't mean that! I meant ... I meant that .... I don't know," she whimpered. "I didn't mean to insult El. I was just carried away by the story."

Zipporah stood and pointed to the flap at the back of the hut. "You must go and take a ritual bath. Cleanse yourself."

"Now? While the guest is telling these wonderful stories? Surely not now? Please Aunt Zippo. Please let me stay. I promise I won't say another word. Please?"

"St … stay," Moshe said, holding up his hand. "Zipporah, Kali mus … must serve, lo?"

Zipporah settled onto her mat again. "Of course, my honorable husband. Your word is supreme in our home." She shook her finger just once at Kaleilah. "Be quiet, then, as you promised. And please refill our drinks."

"But … is it true?" Kaleilah pleaded, as she carefully poured the wine.

Moshe laughed. "Only a little, swee … sweet bird. I ka … killed a mean taskmaster, but I di … didn't mean to ka … kill him. No lie … lightning."

Kaleilah turned to Amichai. "Is Uncle Moshe still wanted for murder there? Is he under a death decree?"

"I thought you weren't going to say another word," Zipporah admonished. "I suppose we might as well try to hush the songbird."

Amichai nodded. "I believe it is still so, though perhaps the Egyptians have forgotten. That was thirty floods past. But we Hebrews will never forget. The Great Moshe lives on in our legends, as strong as Joseph of the many colored coat, and Abraham of the idols. Have you heard those stories?" he asked Kaleilah.

She shook her head, wide eyed. "No! Oh, please tell me. Tell me of Joseph with the many colored coat. Was he rich?"

"He was eventually," Amichai said. "The story begins with his father Jacob, who had twelve children, though he loved Joseph the best."

They stayed up all night, even unto the sun rising, telling stories and discussing life as a slave in Egypt. And in the morning the cattle bellowed, but Moshe slept.

Chapter Three: Moshe Gives Bad News

Zipporah hummed a love song as she knelt behind
Moshe, brushing and clipping his hair. He sat cross-
legged, staring out of the open door at the herd of sheep
grazing on the pasture. The summer sun warmed the
indolent thick alfalfa, providing bountiful fodder for the
healthy animals.

"You have more twigs in your hair than my father
has sheep in the field," she complained, her musical
voice adding humor to the scold. "I made you such a
comfortable bag, yet you still prefer a pile of leaves for
your pillow."

Zipporah waited for Moshe to reply, and when he
didn't, she peeked around at his face. His gaze lay out
the door, unseeing. "What troubles you, my honorable
husband?"

He shook his head.

She rose and returned with a bowl of grapes. "Look,
my love. The grapes have grown plump and sweet. We
will have a bountiful crop, and fresh wonderful wine.
Let me peel a few for your pleasure." She peeled the
first and placed it in his mouth. She leaned forward and
licked the juice dribbling down his chin as he chewed.

"Zipporah, I fa … fear that Yahweh is ca … calling
me."

"Calling you, my husband? I thought you spoke to
him in your prayers. I certainly speak with Yam in
mine."

"No, my la … love. Yahweh calls me ba … back to
Egypt."

She stood up, stumbling into the wall. "Egypt?
Please do not jest in such fashion, my husband. Why
would we leave this wonderful home? My father has put
you in charge of the tribe's largest herd. We have sweet
fruit and lovely wine. My cousin bakes enough bread
for our whole tribe. We want for nothing and have
everything. The great God El, father of Baal and Yam,

has granted peace and prosperity to his son and humble priest, Jethro, my father, and all his sons and daughters."

Zipporah paused to catch her breath, struggling to control the trembling in her hands.

"Zipporah, I honor your fa … father. He has been ka … kind to this str … stranger in a strange land. And yet, E … Egypt calls to me."

Zipporah threw up her hands and raised her face to the top of the tent. "Oh Great El, bring peace and sense to my honorable husband. Banish these thoughts of far away places and bring him contentment."

She turned and looked at him. "What now, my honorable husband? Do you still feel that wanderlust eating at your soul?"

Moshe nodded, and reached out his hand, but Zipporah stepped back. Closing her eyes she sang a wailing prayer, her voice like the mourning dove, pitched in flats and sad resonances. She weaved and danced, singing now loudly, now softly; her sounds echoing across the field. Kaleilah peeked in, and Moshe motioned for her to sit on a pillow inside the door.

Zipporah sang and circled until she collapsed onto a pile of pillows, her head thrust back, her eyes closed, a few sobs shaking her body. Kaleilah rose and brought a jug of water, carefully dripping some onto Zipporah's face and into her mouth.

Zipporah leaned up on her elbow. "What insanity would drive you to drag your family across hundreds of leagues, past bandits and kidnappers, through deserts and wilderness, where even the greatest of guides falls prey to thirst or wild beasts?"

Kaleilah looked at Zipporah wide-eyed, then at Moshe, and back to Zipporah. "A travel? You are going somewhere? How exciting! Please, let me come! I can mind the children."

Zipporah wiped her tears with her sleeve. "You do not want to come on *this* adventure, my sweet Kali. Your Uncle Moshe talks of returning to Egypt."

Kaleilah's eyes grew as big as saucers. She jumped up and ran over to Moshe, kneeling at his feet.

"Oh, my dear uncle. Egypt! The land of the pyramids and the golden calves? I have heard such incredible stories about your magical homeland. Are you really thinking of going there?"

"He is sun struck," Zipporah announced. "The visit from our guest has brought back strange memories." She turned to Moshe. "You can't go back, my honorable husband. They will cut you in quarters and feed your parts to their pigs. They will make me their concubine and enslave our two boys. You are tired. You are confused. I curse this Hebrew who has brought insanity into your heart."

She rose and began pacing again, stopping in front of Kaleilah. "Egypt is not a vacation spot, Kali. It is a place ruled by cruel pharaohs who abuse all for their own pleasures. Nowhere are the people as evil, except for the Sodomites perhaps."

Kaleilah looked from one to the other. She retreated to the pillow by the door, tightly cuddling her legs with her arms.

Moshe nodded. "It is da … dangerous. If I go, I sh … should go alone."

Zipporah knelt before him. "Where you go, my honorable husband, I follow."

Chapter Four: Jethro Predicts Zipproah's Future

"Jethro, my father, I am here."

From her genuflection, Zipporah watched the priest rise from his worshipping. Jethro dipped his fingers in the holy spring and, while chanting a prayer, sprinkled some drops onto his daughter. He bent down and kissed her on the scalp.

"Rise my daughter. What is on your mind?"

Zipporah sat on the bench in the garden temple. "My honorable husband speaks of returning to Egypt, my reverent father."

Jethro sat down next to her. Together they watched the holy water as it poured out from the fissure in the rock. Zipporah had heard Jethro tell that it spouted directly from the mouth of Yam, the goddess of rivers and sea.

"I have spoken to Moshe about this," Jethro said. "He has been having dreams. Some are scenes from his youth, studying science with the Pharaoh's children, or secret visits with his mother. Other times he dreams of the Egypt of today, with the oppression of his people."

"Dreams are like the mist over the morning lake, my reverent father. When the sun rises, they dissipate into the nothingness."

Jethro ran his finger across her brow. "As always, you are the practical one. Would you please bring me some wine?"

Zipporah hurried to the altar. She bowed before the statue of El before retrieving the small vessel her father kept there. Jethro murmured a blessing over it and took a light sip. She knelt on the floor at his feet.

"Do you remember that terrible storm last moon, my daughter?" he asked.

"Yes, of course. Lightning and thunder crashed like Gods at war. We all huddled close together all night."

"Did you notice Moshe leave for a bit?"

She thought back to that night, the two boys cuddling in fright beside her. "Um ... maybe. Yes, I remember now. Moshe went out for a few minutes to check on the sheep."

"Something happened to him while he was outside – something he's shared only with me."

Zipporah studied her father's face, his expression calm, ever the reassuring priest. "Moshe has kept a secret from me?"

"He did not wish to frighten you." Jethro reached out and took his daughter's hand, pulling her onto the stone bench beside him. She leaned her head onto his chest and he stroked her hair, bringing to her mind the comforting he used to give when she was a child. She closed her eyes, devoting her full attention to his words.

"He told me he had a strange experience that night. While he was out in the storm, a lightning bolt struck a bush near him. It burst into flame, sizzling and roaring with a voice that sounded almost human. As he stared into the flames, he beheld a vision of his God, Yahweh. He felt a calling to return to help his family and his people."

Zipporah rose and walked to the fountain of Yam where she bent forward and splashed her face, trying to hide the tears running down her cheeks.

"It is the fault of this fellow he met in town, this Amichai. He flatters my husband with nonsense, stories of adventure and ambition. Moshe is not the youth of twenty who stood up to a taskmaster. If he returns to Egypt he will be killed. We will all be killed." She buried her face in her hands. "Oh Father, what can I do?"

Jethro rose and came to his daughter, squatting by her side. She snuggled up to him as he put his arm across her shoulder. His odor brought back memories of her childhood.

"Do you know what his name means, this Amichai?" he asked.

She shook her head.

"It means 'my people are alive.' You see, not only is he a messenger, but also his name is a message. Clearly

Moshe's Yahweh delivered Amichai from Egyptian bondage and directed him to our door."

Zipporah began sobbing again and Jethro rubbed her back gently. "We have a lovely and comfortable life here," she pleaded. "I have birthed two of your favorite grandchildren. Moshe is one of the best shepherds in the tribe, keeping your sheep fed and safe. Please, my reverent father, order him to stay here, where he is needed, where he belongs."

Jethro stood and walked to the statue of El, where he bowed and muttered a near silent prayer. He returned to where Zipporah sat, and placing his hands on her head he kissed her gently on the scalp.

"Though I am a priest of El, I can not claim to understand the ways of Gods. Moshe believes that Yahweh is calling him back to Egypt. What can I say to him that would make a difference, my sweet dove? When the Gods have spoken, man must bow and obey."

Zipporah began wailing, falling prostrate on the ground and rubbing her face in the dirt. "Oh, my reverent father, can you possibly see any good from all this? If Yahweh is calling Moshe to return to Egypt, will he protect him? Will he protect me and our children?"

Jethro reached into a bag he held at his side, pulling out a small collection of bones. He shook them lightly, their rattles creating an accompaniment to Zipporah's sad song, until she stopped and looked up at him.

"My fortune?" she asked.

"Yes. I will throw a spread and we will see what El will reveal."

Jethro lowered himself to the ground, cross-legged, his joints creaking with the effort. Zipporah drew a triangle in the dirt, murmuring "Baal and Yam at the base, El to rule above." She sat cross-legged at its apex.

He held his arms high, old flesh jiggling from his underarms as he shook. He spilled the half dozen bone pieces into the holy triangle, making a scattering of strange shapes and design. Zipporah watched him study them, nodding, and then shaking his head.

"What do you see, my reverent father?"

"Moshe will be drawn into great events in Egypt, Zipporah. I have never seen such a powerful stack in all my many tosses. Great events, Zipporah, great events."

"And what of me and my sons? What do you see of us?"

Jethro reached forward and scooped up the bones, placing them back in their bag. He reached out his arms, palms upwards. "Help me up, my daughter."

She rose quickly to her feet and pulled him up. Jethro tottered for a moment and she handed him his staff. He put both hands on its head, raised his face to the ivy covered arbor above, and chanted a prayer. Zipporah bowed her head and waited patiently. When he stopped chanting, Zipporah looked up to find his gaze fixed on her.

"I know you will try to accompany your husband, my dutiful daughter, and that is how it should be. But Egypt is not to be your fate. I foresee you living here, being a comfort to me in my old age."

Zipporah felt her face flush. "Where goeth my husband, there goeth I! May no God stand in my way!"

Jethro shook his head.

She collapsed to her knees at her father's feet, grabbing his legs. "Say it isn't so, my reverent father. Do not deliver me to such a betrayal."

She groveled before him, kissing his feet over, washing them with her tears. "I *will* follow him. I swear to El and Baal and Yam. I swear even to Yahweh if that is what it will take. I *will* be with my husband. Unless the Gods force me to retreat, where Moshe leads, I will follow."

She didn't look up to hear Jethro say softly, "Then we must leave it in their hands, my daughter."

Chapter Five: The Journey Begins

The sun hadn't topped the eastern mountains as the travelers gathered at the tribal clearing to make their farewells. Many of Zipporah's cousins lay asleep from the party of the night before. Her sisters and sisters-in-law gathered around her, hugging and kissing her farewell.

Zipporah gave the last one a hug and walked over to where Jethro talked with Moshe.

"Moshe," he said. "You have a long and dangerous journey ahead of you."

"'Tis only a moo … moon," Moshe replied.

Jethro shook his head. "It will be twice that or more before you reach Giza, of this I'm sure. I wish to give you a parting gift, something magical you might find useful."

Moshe bowed his head and kissed Jethro's hand. "Your ble … blessings are my gi … gift, Father."

"Those you have, my son. Here, though, is a gift worthy of he who hopes to lead his people out of bondage. You will take my magical staff."

The priest held up his staff, showing to Moshe what looked like nothing more than a carved wooden stick. Jethro shouted and gave it a shake. The stick began moving, undulating. Jethro threw it to the ground and it became a python, hissing and writhing. Zipporah and Moshe jumped back in alarm.

Jethro laughed and held his arm to the ground. The python curled up around it and hung playfully around his neck. Jethro fed it a small piece of meat.

"This is Sheeba. Look here at this cradle I've made. It's a thin curved bamboo that lies straight when Sheeba's resting in it. But when I shake her to the ground, the cradle springs back into my hand. It looks like my staff has magically turned into a snake. I give Sheeba and her cradle to you as my parting gift."

Moshe kneeled and kissed his father-in-law's feet. "Th ... thank you my reverent fa ... father. I tr ... treasure your ga ... gift and your blessings."

Jethro placed his hands above Moshe and chanted. "May the blessings of El be watching over you and your family on this and all your passages, my son. May the strong hand of Baal direct you upon paths of stealth and fortitude. May the kiss of Yam bring you sustenance. And may the sharp eye of Yahweh bring you the success you both so desire.

"It is usually only in death that we make such heavy farewells, Moshe of the Hebrews. Although bereaved at your parting, I will be comforted in knowing that you go with a strong heart and a clean spirit."

He leaned down and kissed Moshe once more.

"In your language, Shalom, go in peace, my son. Perhaps the Gods may one day reunite you with those here who love you. And if not here, may you find some other land of milk and honey for you and your people."

Zipporah stepped up to her father who took her bent head in both of his hands. "May the blessings of El be upon you and your group. May Yam, the guardian of women and children, keep a special eye on you, my daughter, and upon thy children, and upon all your group."

"Thank you, my reverent father."

"I have a parting gift for you as well," he said, handing her a small waxed vessel. "I have sealed some holy water from the fountain of Yam. It will heal illness of the stomach. Use it wisely."

"Gershom! Eliezer!" At his call, his two grandsons came running up to the old priest.

"Yes, Papa?" Gershom asked. His spindly body showed the tan of many days played out in the summer sunshine. His little brother toddled up beside them, laughing, holding up a turtle he had caught for his grandfather to see.

"My children, you are about to depart on a great adventure. Obey your elders and stay out of trouble."

He smiled at Kaleilah who had come up slowly. "Ah, my granddaughter of the never-ending questions plans to join this little crew too? Does your mother approve of these plans?"

Kaleilah shrugged. "I am almost of twelve summers, Papa. It is time I saw a little of this great world, don't you think? Have you ever been to Giza, Papa? Have you ever seen the Great Sphinx or bathed in the mighty Nile? I hear it is so wide that one can stand on one bank and not see the far side! Could that be true, Papa?"

Zipporah watched her father smile.

"I guess you'll have to see for yourself, sweet child," he said. "Your Uncle Moshe knows the way. He knows to cross the Great Reed Sea when the tides have run it dry, before the water returns in a flood, crashing upon itself in a thunderous tumult. He knows how to hide and when to run. He knows where he is going and why."

The priest paused, and Zipporah watched him catch a tear on his sleeve.

He raised his arms above his head, reaching for the skies above. "So, I say to you all, may the Gods speed you upon your journeys, and may all your fortunes be happy ones."

He waved to Amichai who had stayed back, holding the two donkeys loaded with the provisions. The others joined the Hebrew, and the group headed off to the west, turning at the top of the hill to wave goodbye.

"Will we ever see Papa again?" Gershom asked his mother.

Zipporah bent down and kissed him, her tears falling upon his dark curly hair. "We must leave that in the hands of El, my son."

Chapter Six: Moshe Becomes Ill

Near dusk of the second day the travelers came to a small inn where they rented a room for the night as the only guests. Moshe negotiated with the keeper, a silver coin sufficient for food for the six of them and oats for their pack animals. The keeper told them, while there was still light they could bathe in the small river that ran in back of the building. Moshe asked Amichai to take the boys out for the swim, so Kaleilah could stay with Zipporah and himself.

"I'm ta … tired," Moshe said. "I think I'll pa … pass on the evening ma … meal and get some ra … rest."

Zipporah looked at him in alarm. "You looked flushed, my honorable husband. Let me feel of your brow." She touched him and drew her hand back sharply. "You are with fever, my love. Quickly, let us put you to bed and bring you water."

Moshe lay on the straw pallet, took one sip of the water, and vomited. Through the night and the next day he continued with vomiting and diarrhea, fever and sweating. The diarrhea became copious, and though he was able to keep down a tiny bit of water and grape juice, his eyes became sunken and his heart raced.

Zipporah sat by his bedside, keeping him clean, wiping his brow, encouraging him to sip the fluids. Kaleilah and Amichai kept the boys busy, and took turns relieving Zipporah. By midnight of the second day Moshe became delirious. The boys were asleep, the other three sat at his bedside.

"He's going to die, isn't he?" Kaleilah asked.

"Truly, one can never understand the purposes of God." Amichai said. "Yet I can not believe that Yahweh delivered me unto Midian to find and fetch The Great Moshe, just to strike him down on the journey to liberation. There must be a message here, something that Yahweh is trying to tell us."

Zipporah glared at him. "Who is this Yahweh that wishes to kill my husband? Moshe is a good man, a kind father, generous to his slaves, obedient to his elders. Why would Yahweh want to kill him? Wasn't the whole purpose of this expedition to do your Yahweh's bidding?"

The three sat in silence, listening to Moshe mutter and moan. Kaleilah mopped his brow while Zipporah urged him to sip on a cup of wine.

"Let us consider," Amichai said. "For the past thirty cycles, Moshe has lived under the protection of El, the God of Midian. Now that he has left that land, Yahweh once more has control. Clearly, Yahweh is angry with Moshe."

"Yahweh has no grounds to be angry with his servant Moshe," Zipporah said. "Even under the roof of El, Moshe kept true to his home beliefs."

"That's true," Kaleilah piped in. "He has all sorts of strange beliefs. He won't eat any of the delicious roast pig, or the little shelled river creatures. Why do you have such rules, Amichai?"

Amichai shrugged. "I can not answer why God asks these things of us."

"Moshe has us partake of all types of rituals," Zipporah said. "He has his prayers for the little box on the doorway, and his prayers for the wine and the bread. One must make allowances for those who grew up in strange lands. I have always honored his peculiar beliefs and he has respected mine."

Silence descended on the sad group, interrupted by Moshe's moans and occasional incoherent mutter.

"It's true that my people have many different rituals," Amichai said quietly. "We call these 'Yahweh's commandments.' And some may seem peculiar, as you point out. But there is one commandment that is more important than all others, one that we use to identify all the males of our people. I fear that it is this very commandment that has angered

Yahweh, that has brought his wrath upon The Great Moshe."

Zipporah sat back, fanning herself. The smell of Moshe's illness and the heat of the closed-in room seemed oppressive, even with the cooling of the night air. "What failed deed or indiscretion do you blame this illness on?" she asked.

Amichai pointed to the pallet with the two boys. "I have been swimming with your sons. Gershom has undergone the required Hebrew ritual. Not so for Eliezer. I believe that Yahweh is bringing his vengeance upon Moshe for disobeying this commandment."

Zipporah stood up, stomped in a circle, and spat upon Amichai. "Take that for your Hebrew rituals. After inflicting such damage upon Gershom, I shouted and ranted and swore that Moshe would never again torture one of my little boys. No. Never, I say! Moshe is the master of our home, but I am the mother of my children. I will *not* let you cut on my baby's penis."

Amichai wiped the spit off his hair, but did not look away from Moshe. "Then you condemn your husband to death."

Zipporah tilted her head back and screamed. "Noooo!"

In the early morning hours, when all others lay asleep, Zipporah broke the seal on the bottle of holy water and eased it to Moshe's lips. She allowed one small swallow to trickle into his mouth, about half the container, before resealing the vessel and hiding it away.

Chapter Seven: Circumcision

"It's been a full night and most of a day since Uncle Moshe last spoke, Aunt Zipporah," Kaleilah said, standing behind the grieving woman and massaging her neck. "His breathing is shallow and his skin white as the goose's down. Is there a place where the soul goes after death?"

Zipporah sang a prayer unto Yam, the healer. Her voice rose and fell in low-toned trills, bouncing off the walls in harmonic echoes. When she finished she murmured, "The innkeeper says Moshe has dysentery. If he survives another day or two he should recover. So says the innkeeper."

"That is nothing but a self-fulfilling prophecy," Amichai said. "The innkeeper will be right either way. I put my trust in Yahweh."

"And I put mine in El, Baal, and Yam," Zipporah replied.

"Really?" Amichai said with clear sarcasm. "So far your Gods have failed you. Perhaps it's time to try something different ... before it's too late."

Zipporah leaned forward and shook Moshe. Surprisingly his eyes opened. "Moshe? Moshe, my love, can you hear me?"

He turned and looked at her. "Yahweh is ka ... calling me home, my wa ... wife. I have not ma ... much longer on this earth."

"Why, why, why? Oh, Moshe, tell me. Why does Yahweh hate you?"

Moshe stared at her ... through her, as if seeing something deep inside, or in another world. A beam of light from the setting sun snaked through a crack in the walls and lit up his mouth. His lips were so dry his voice cracked as he tried to speak. "I have dis ... disobeyed." He closed his eyes and a shudder ran through him. Zipporah thought he had passed and screamed, "NO!" But he took another raspy breath, then another, and when she placed a pomegranate between his lips he sucked upon it.

Zipporah turned to Amichai, her face stretched in sadness. "What if I subject my little Eliezer to this cruel cutting, and still Moshe dies?"

Amichai shrugged. "I can not answer that, honorable lady. Yet I have had another thought I must share. If Moshe survives and we arrive in Giza with his son unfixed, the people will not accept him as their savoir. How could he be Yahweh's servant if he so clearly disobeys His commandments?"

Zipporah nodded and rose, indicating for Kaleilah to accompany her through the back door that led to the river. There she called Eliezer to her from his play. She bade him drink the cup of wine she had brought. When he had fallen under its touch, she sang a prayer to Baal, he who brought stones upon the earth, who looked to the fortunes of men. With a shout she ran the sharp stone across her son's foreskin. He screamed in pain, the blood spurting across her arms, face, and gown. She bade Kaleilah to hold the sea moss she had gathered against his sore and to comfort him.

Taking the foreskin back into the sickroom, she rubbed it across Moshe's brow, leaving a bloody mark, and threw it at his feet.

"Surely thou art a bloody husband of mine now," she swore. She sang a soft mourning song for the impending death of her husband. Holding the vial of holy water to Moshe's lips, she drained out the last drop. She slumped across his chest, falling into a deep sleep.

Chapter Eight: Moshe Recovers

Zipporah woke to find Moshe sitting up and taking
fluids. "Good ma … morning, my loving wa … wife. I
am ba … better."
She jumped up and hugged him, kissing him
repeatedly on his face and chest.
"Oh, Moshe, my love, you have returned to me. I
thought you had passed over, yet now you are alive. So
alive! Praise be to Yam and her wondrous holy water!"
Amichai shushed her. "Don't insult Yahweh, most
honorable lady. It is by His hand that The Great Moshe
has been delivered from death."
"According to you, it was His hand that put him in
such dire need. And at what cost, to what purpose? Just
so I had to torture my little boy, a mere lad barely upon
his third summer. What type of God demands such
pain? Where is my little Eliezer? I will see him."
"Over here, Aunt Zipporah," Kaleilah called. "The
bleeding has stopped, but he is swollen and sore."
Zipporah went to the pallet where her son lay curled
up, holding his hands over his genitals. Tears filled his
eyes.
"It hurts, Mommy."
She gently moved his hands away, biting her lips on
seeing the red swollen penis. She bent down and kissed
his forehead.
She turned to Moshe, defiance in her voice. "We
must return to my father's home right away," she said.
"Jethro has medicines and prayer that can save this
child. We leave within the hour."
Moshe nodded slowly. "You spee … speak truth,
Zipporah. You four mus … must return now. Amichai
and I wi … will carry on."
Zipporah stomped and wailed. "You can not send us
away, my honorable husband. You must give up this ill-
fated adventure and return with me to your loving home.
Return to the protection of the kind and generous El.
Return to our home where you have shelter, a wife, and

a loving family. Return with us to the riches we have beyond our needs. Truly, hasn't El provided you with everything your heart could desire?"

Moshe slowly shook his head. "I can not tur … turn back my love. Though my heart is br … breaking into a thou … thousand pa … pa … pieces, I mu … must send you ba … back to your father."

Zipporah flung away her robe and knelt naked in front of her husband. Amichai turned his face to the wall.

"My husband, I beg of you. Look upon your wife, I, who have borne your children, who have acquiesced to your every wish, even to the mutilation of my own innocent children. Even to this final act which may yet cost us the life of our loving son, I have been your servant. I plead in full supplication, my honorable husband. Do not cast me away like some soiled robe of which you've grown tired." She wailed and wept, her tears pouring a river upon the dirt floor.

Moshe stared at the ceiling, his prayers drifting upwards. "I mu … must be true to my ga … God. I know that des … destiny awaits me in Gi … Giza, my love. I mus … must go on without you."

Zipporah knelt, crying until no more tears would come, no more sobs shake her body. She finally fell back on her haunches and wrapped the robe Kaleilah brought around herself.

"Truly I do not understand how you can honor a God so cruel."

She received no response. Shaking herself, she stood and turned to Kaleilah.

"Come, Kali. Gather all of our bags. The sooner we get on the road the better. We will try to walk deep into the evening. Call Gershom."

As she walked Zipporah kept glancing back to the inn until the images of Moshe and Amichai standing, watching them go, disappeared in the rolling landscape of the prairie.

Gershom pulled on his mother's hand. "Will we ever see father again?"

Zipporah shook her head. "Yahweh is a jealous God, jealous of the kindness of our El. He has stripped Moshe of all that he loves. From this journey there will be no return."

The End

Author's Notes, "Esau"

Esau's wives: There are different interpretations of Esau's marriages. I based this version on Genesis 36:2; Esau took his wives from the daughters of Canaan: Adah the daughter of Elon the Hittite and Oholibamah the daughter of Anah and the granddaughter of Zibeon the Hivite; also Basemath, Ishmael's daughter, the sister of Nebaioth. Adah bore Eliphaz to Esau, and Basemath bore Reuel, and Oholibamah bore Jeush and Jalam and Korah. These are the sons of Esau who were born to him in the land of Canaan.

This is in contrast to information from Genesis 26:34, which states; When Esau was forty years old, he married Judith daughter of Beeri the Hittite, and also Basemath daughter of Elon the Hittite.

The reference to marrying Ishmael's daughter comes from Genesis 28:9; So he went to Ishmael and married Mahalath, the sister of Nebaioth and daughter of Ishmael son of Abraham, in addition to the wives he already had.

In "Esau," Chapter Nine, Eliphaz tells Esau that Jacob's sons have sold one brother into Egyptian slavery. In actual time sequence, this occurs later, in Genesis 37. In fact, Genesis 33:2 states that Jacob placed Rachel and Joseph in the back of his group when the two clans met. This change is for dramatic effect.

There are a few mentions of metal in the story, mostly cauldrons and knives. Historians place the first use of simple metals, usually copper, about 6000 B.C.E., so roughly 8000 years ago. Hebrew scholars count Day 1 from the time of Abraham. Currently the Hebrew year is about 5760. Consequently, the story of Esau occurred about 2400 years after the invention of metal, and Zipporah's story four hundred years later. Zipporah used flint instead of metal to circumcise her son out of tradition.

Author Notes on "Zipporah"

Moses kisses the scroll by the door. The Mezuzah is a hand written Hebrew prayer in Hebrew, the Shemah, which says, "Hear Israel, the Lord is our God, the Lord is one." Found in Deuteronomy, which chronologically postdates Exodus (the Moses story), scholars believe this concept was first proclaimed by Moses. In Deuteronomy 6:9, as well as 11:20, the Jewish people are commanded, "...you shall write them on the doorposts of your house and upon your gates."

you shall love your God, believe only in Him, keep His commandments, and pass all of this on to your children.

Gershom and Eliezer join Moses and the Hebrews later in the desert and their descendants become Levi scholars; treasurers and temple keepers. Zipporah later appears with her father Jethro and her two children in Exodus Chapter 18 when he comes to visit Moses after the exodus of the children of Israel from Egypt. It is not known what happened to Zipporah past this point; she might have stayed with Moses until her death, for Miriam and Aaron complain about the Ethiopian woman he married in Numbers Chapter 12, or she may have returned to Midian with her father.

These two quotes come from the story of Exodus: "Stranger in a strange land" (Exodus 2:22) and "Bloody husband of mine" (Exodus 4:25)

About the Author:

Philip L. Levin, MD, comes from a literary family. His mother, Beatrice S. Levin, published thirty books and over a thousand articles. His father, Dr. Franklyn K. Levin, served as editor of Geophysics Magazine, as well as publishing a slew of his own scientific articles. Philip has been a writer since childhood. While in medical school, for example, his publications earned him enough to pay for his tuition, so that he graduated debt free.

"Altered Perspectives" is Philip's thirteenth published book, following his suspense thriller "Inheritance," a series of four "Afternoon Tales" anthologies, a series of audiobooks, and two children's photo books, "Consuto and the Rain God," and "Ndovu the Elephant." His writing has won many awards, including RWA Grand Prizes, Poetry accolades, and short story prizes. He serves as president of the 150 member Gulf Coast Writers Association.

For the past thirty-five years Dr. Levin has worked full time as an emergency medicine physician. He travels extensively, including frequent medical missionary trips. He supervised the refurbishing of a hospital in rural Kenya and takes his family on world explorations.

Contact him at writerpllevin@gmail.com or through his website: www.DoctorsDreams.net

17581515R00052

Made in the USA
Charleston, SC
18 February 2013